SHOCK
MARRIAGE FOR
THE POWERFUL
SPANIARD

SHOCK MARRIAGE FOR THE POWERFUL SPANIARD

CATHY WILLIAMS

MILLS & BOON

First published in Great Britain 2019
by Mills & Boon, an imprint of HarperCollins*Publishers*
1 London Bridge Street, London, SE1 9GF

Large Print edition 2020

© 2019 Cathy Williams

ISBN: 978-0-263-08404-7

MIX
Paper from
responsible sources
FSC™ C007454

This book is produced from independently certified FSC™ paper to ensure responsible forest management. For more information visit www.harpercollins.co.uk/green.

Printed and bound in Great Britain
by CPI Group (UK) Ltd, Croydon, CR0 4YY

CHAPTER ONE

'BUT…ANYWAY… I'M glad you've come, Rafael. I wasn't sure whether you would have the time, with this deal you're working on. The newspapers are full of it. It's nice that you still can find a window for a dying old man.'

Rafael raised both eyebrows and looked at his godfather wryly.

David Dunmore might look the very soul of benevolence, with his round spectacles and his tufting grey hair and his jolly, might-almost-be-related-to-Father-Christmas appearance, but Rafael knew very well that behind that façade there beat the heart of someone as sharp as a tack and not averse to a little emotional black-mail.

He also knew that his godfather would never have requested his presence if it hadn't been something urgent. The more convoluted the road he took to get there, the more significant the request would be and right now, after an hour of going round the houses, the size of the favour had increased exponentially.

Rafael relaxed back in his chair, drink in his hand, and braced himself for the long haul.

He hadn't been to his godfather's house in a while. At least a couple of months and not since the old man had been confined to bed and climbing the four walls. When they met, they generally met at the old-fashioned gentleman's club David was a member of where, as he was fond of saying, a chap could hear himself think over a decent whisky and food that hadn't been tampered with by a celebrity chef. 'Cabbage and cottage pie—who needs it?' Rafael would routinely retort, both comfortable in a relationship in which easy familiarity was the offspring of mutual respect and great love.

Rafael had almost forgotten how exquisite this house in Belgravia was, with its graceful proportions and expensive clutter that harked back to a time before minimalism had become the fashion. Soft Persian rugs covered the rich, wooden floor and artefacts from trips abroad jostled with priceless works of art and dainty sculptures.

'I thought you'd stopped playing the "dying" card,' he said mildly. 'After the consultant gave you the all clear and declared you as fit as a fiddle.'

'What do consultants know?'

'A lot, considering the years they've spent practising medicine. Hillman, as it happens, is top of his field when it comes to dodgy tickers, so it's fair to say if he's given you the all clear then the "dying" card is no longer appropriate.'

'Well, superficially I may look as though I'm on the mend, but you have no idea the sort of stress I've been enduring for the past few months.'

The smile dropped from Rafael's face. 'Freddy? Throwing his weight around again? Let me take care of the bloody man.'

'You can't. You have no pull in my company and threatening him with hell and damnation isn't going to work. Right now, he can tell that I've been mortally wounded. I no longer have the stamina or the interest to go into my offices nearly as much as I used to, and he's been...

making mischief. But you know how it is, Rafael. He is my stepson, for better or for worse, and he's also a significant shareholder thanks to the divorce settlement. There is nothing I can do about him, but three of my trusted directors have handed in their resignations, and I fear he is systematically going to try and get his cronies in to replace them. Five years ago, I would have had the energy to keep more of an eye on the boy, but…'

He sighed. 'The old guard are ready to go. They're just allowing themselves to be pushed out slightly ahead of schedule. But that's by the by. For the time being. No, I asked you here to discuss something entirely different.'

Rafael said nothing. His antennae were picking up undercurrents swirling beneath the surface. The silence stretched and then, eventually, David Dunmore reached into the old-fashioned briefcase on the walnut coffee table next to him and extracted an envelope.

He leant forward, handed it to Rafael and then sat back, linking fingers on his protruding stomach to watch his godson with keen interest.

'What's this?'

'Read it.'

Rafael met his godfather's steady gaze, his dark eyes veiled, revealing nothing of the sudden cool chill of apprehension sweeping through him. He opened the envelope. One sheet of paper. It was almost a shock to see that it was a handwritten letter because nowadays nearly everyone communicated by email. The writing was decisive, indicating someone with a strong will, and loopy, indicating that its author was probably a woman.

He felt his godfather's eyes on him, and knew that a response was going to be required, but as he read the letter, then reread it for good measure, for once in his life Rafael found himself at a complete loss for words.

'I know you're probably a little surprised at the content.'

'A *little surprised*? That's the understatement of the century! When did this bombshell drop on your lap and how much is it going to cost you?'

'Now, now, don't jump to conclusions, Rafael. First of all, it's true.' David sighed and sat back and closed his eyes for a few seconds, then he looked at his godson. 'I met Maria Suarez over twenty years ago when I was in my late forties. She was just twenty-six and the most beautiful woman I'd ever laid eyes on. At the time, I was between wives.' He grimaced. 'Shelling out a small fortune in alimony to Fiona and pretty jaded when it came to the opposite sex. Maria was…a breath of fresh air.'

'Okay,' Rafael said crisply. 'Before you start waxing lyrical about beautiful women and breaths of fresh air, David, let's cut to the chase.' The urge to protect—a primal force that harked back down the years to a time when this man sitting in front of him had been his safe harbour in turbulent waters—kicked into gear with a vengeance.

'This woman, if it even *is* her, gets in touch with you to tell you that you have a long-lost kid on the other side of the world. Says she's about to kick the bucket and her conscience has got the better of her.' He clicked his tongue with rampant disbelief. 'Question—how does she know where you live? And presumably, if she knows where you live, then she also knows how wealthy you are.'

David shifted uncomfortably and shot his godson a jaundiced look.

'How did you meet her?'

Long-lost daughter...? Presumably as poor as a church mouse...? In need of some cash...? And that was if there was any daughter at all and if the mysterious letter-writer was who she claimed to be! Could this tender and touching story have any more holes?

And, if his godfather was inclined to believe all this tosh, then it was up to Rafael to rescue him from his folly. There was no way he was going to allow any more potential gold-diggers to run roughshod over him and the 'prodigal daughter' angle was just the sort of cunning ploy his godfather would fall for. *Was* falling for, from the looks of it.

'I was in Argentina all those years ago,' David reflected with the sort of wistful expression that made Rafael want to grind his teeth together in frustration. 'Out there for a year, sourcing locations for my flagship South American boutique hotels, introducing them to the concept of the eco hotel. Met her when I was there. My word, what a raven-haired beauty. As sweet-natured as it was possible to be. I fell head over heels in love with her.'

'But no happy ending.' Rafael yanked him back to reality. 'Considering you returned to London and promptly married Ingrid and kissed sweet goodbye to yet another sizeable chunk of your assets when you divorced her— not to mention bidding farewell to the shares in the company which your dear stepson is intent on taking over.' He sighed. 'And you still haven't answered my question. How does this woman, if she is who she claims to be, know where you live?'

'She could easily have contacted me via any one of my hotels—and let's not forget the Internet, dear boy. There's no such thing as privacy any more.'

'And yet here you are. No raven-haired beauty to be seen for miles and never has been. So what happened?'

'I was called away on an urgent family matter. Had to leave without warning, practically in the dead of night. Mother had been rushed to hospital with a heart attack. Left a message with Antonio, who was my right-hand guy over there at the time. Told him to explain… Well, got back and she'd absconded. Turned out she felt she wasn't good enough for me, that our worlds were too far apart, felt that she would end up holding me back—even though I never, not once, gave any hint that that was or ever would be the case. Obviously didn't feel as strongly about me as I felt about her. Wasn't prepared to give it a go. It broke my heart, Rafael. Broke my heart.'

'Worlds too far apart…hmm. And her world was…?'

'She worked as the chambermaid in the hotel where I was based while I oversaw work on my buildings. She was the love of my life, Rafael, and now…now, from nowhere… I receive this letter telling me that I have a daughter. My own flesh and blood.'

Rafael didn't say anything. Chambermaid? Had his godfather really thought that he could hitch his wagon to someone who worked as a chambermaid? Not that a chambermaid could have been any worse than the horror with whom he had eventually tied the knot, an Amazonian Swede who had taken him for everything she could get her hands on when, three years post-walking up the aisle, the marriage had fallen apart in a welter of acrimony and infidelity on her part. Not only had she left with a juicy injection of cash and three houses, but she'd also managed to wangle a tasty chunk of shares for her useless son. His godfather was still paying the price for that particular mad dash down the aisle in search of love.

'I'm filling in the blanks,' David continued, voice rising in direct proportion to his excitement now that the cat was out of the bag. 'I think she ran away, just disappeared, but returned to her place of birth at some point because that's where the girl is. Working as a nanny for an expat couple in the suburbs.'

Rafael didn't say anything because he didn't know where this was leading. Eventually, he asked neutrally, 'Have you had a DNA test done?'

David bristled. 'The timing works.'

'Don't believe what you want to believe.'

'And I won't approach the situation ready to assume that it's dead in the water before it's begun.'

'Okay.' Rafael sighed and ran his fingers through his hair. 'So have you contacted the woman? The daughter?'

'Maria has passed away.' His eyes clouded. 'That much I do know. I've naturally set in motion the standard enquiries. I've got sufficient information at my disposal to contact my daughter and I've had enough time to figure out...the way forward when it comes to doing that.'

'Long-haul flight to Argentina?' Rafael looked at his godfather, whose head was tilted to one side while his mind played with the abundance of revelations that unexpectedly had been dumped on his plate. 'You'll have to check with the consultant. You don't need another heart scare.' Something inside twisted at the thought of that, a mixture of fear and panic.

'It was more than a scare!'

'Tell me why I'm here, David,' Rafael coaxed gently. 'As a confidante to this information or for some other purpose?'

'I can't go to Argentina—but you can, my dear boy, and you must.' He sat forward, as serious as Rafael had ever seen him 'I'll make it worth your while...'

Sofia Suarez impatiently tapped her foot and stared out towards the imposing wrought-iron gates that protected the owners of this fabulous property from any strays who might decide to drop in to see whether they might be in luck with handouts.

In this exclusive enclave on the outskirts of Buenos Aires, the wealthy always made sure that they were well protected, rarely opening their doors to anyone they didn't know.

They had enough money to make sure that hired help took care of whatever they considered beneath them. Which, she thought now—tapping her foot ever-quicker and checking her watch—was why she was here, waiting for the appearance of a gardener who should have showed up an hour and a half earlier.

James and Elizabeth Walters were off skiing with their two young children.

'No idea why we've been landed with this gardener chap when I've been perfectly happy getting a team in once a week,' James had complained to her a week earlier, when he had appeared in the doorway of her bedroom without any advance warning. 'But my boss has asked me to take the man on as a favour for a friend in London. Anyway, Lizzy and I won't be around, so you're going to have to show him the ropes.'

'Yes, of course, although you did say that this would be allotted holiday time for me,' Sofia had said, taking a deep breath and counting to ten. James and Elizabeth Walters were very, very fond of dictating exactly what she did with her free time, even though her hours were clearly stated in the job-acceptance form she had signed a year ago.

But she needed this job. The pay was fantastic and she had paid upfront for her online accountancy course. It hadn't been cheap and, added to that the fact that she tried to help out financially with her aunt, well, unless she won the lottery she was pretty much stuck. Someone in debt was not someone holding any trump cards.

'We were more than understanding when you had to interrupt your working hours to visit your mother in the hospital,' her boss had retorted without batting an eyelid. 'So, grounds for complaint? Don't think so. We're going to be gone for a fortnight. You're going to be twiddling your thumbs, and getting damn well paid for it, so I don't see where the problem is.'

He had raked his eyes over her in that insolent way that bordered on sexual harassment and stared narrowly. 'The man is only going to be here for a month at the most. Some nonsense about him needing money while he bums his way around South America. God only knows why these types don't find decent jobs like everyone else but I have no choice in the matter.'

He'd straightened and stared at her for a few seconds longer than was comfortable and Sofia had done what she always did when her boss made her feel uncomfortable—she gritted her teeth and stared down silently at the floor until he lost interest.

Which he had, having reminded her of the thousand other things she was charged to do in their absence, from sorting out the gardener to cleaning the proverbial silverware. So, *twiddling her thumbs*? What a joke. That was the one thing she could never be accused of having done and certainly not when she was staring at a list of instructions.

The blazing sun was sinking into a violet sky when, finally, the intercom went and a disembodied voice announced the arrival of the gardener.

'You're late,' Sofia said, not bothering to mince her words. The man had spoken in English and she had replied in same. A nomadic life had made her fluent in it and it helped that the people currently employing her refused to speak Spanish. 'I've been hanging around waiting for you to show up for the past two hours.'

She could scarcely make out the figure on the visual display. She was keen to get him in and out of her way because she had a busy evening lined up with her accountancy books. It was hard enough finding the time to study without wasting precious hours with her ear to the buzzer.

'Who am I talking to?'

'This is Señorita Suarez and I'm to show you the ropes while the Walters are away.' There was a brief pause, and for some reason Sofia felt the hairs on the back of her neck stand on end, but the moment passed—to be replaced with mounting irritation, because a minute in and the man was already beginning to get on her nerves.

'Are you going to let me in?'

Sofia bristled. 'I will need to ask you some security questions.'

'Why?'

'Excuse me?'

'Why?' Rafael repeated.

Sofia looked around her at the massively expensive furnishings. *'El señor de la casa,'* she intoned with saccharin sweetness, 'is a little cautious when it comes to allowing strangers into his house. He's fond of his possessions remaining on the premises.'

'El señor,' Rafael drawled in response, 'has nothing to fear. I very much doubt there's a single thing he possesses that I could possibly want.' He held up the introductory letter David had handed over to him some days ago. He had barely been able to contain his amusement at the thought of his high-powered and much-feared godson slumming it with a lawn mower and taking orders from someone he

didn't know. 'Peer carefully and you'll be able to see that I am exactly who I say I am. Name is Rafael and I'm here to look after *el señor*'s garden for a couple of weeks. Rest assured, I won't be leaving with his lawn mower and the pruning shears.'

'You're Spanish?'

'So it would seem. Now, open the gate. I've spent hours travelling. It's been a hellish trip. I'm hot and tired and I'm not prepared to spend the next half an hour sweltering out here while I answer pointless questions that don't need to be asked.'

Sofia could scarcely believe what she was hearing. For one very wicked moment, she almost wished that James and his stuck-up wife were here so that they could experience a cocky, arrogant hired hand who wasn't afraid to speak his mind.

But they weren't, because they were busy having fun on the slopes. No, *she* was here, working, as always, beyond her brief. She buzzed open the iron gates and waited until she heard the sharp ring of the doorbell, immediately followed by the thundering of the lionhead brass knocker, as though the man outside couldn't wait the seconds it might take her to answer the door.

She sprinted and yanked open the front door, letting in the fragrant smell of grass and trees and the soothing orchestra of twilight insects, and then stopped dead in her tracks.

Just for a few seconds. Just as she registered the guy towering in front of her, his hand raised as though about to bang the knocker again.

Drop-dead gorgeous. The breath left her in a whoosh, as though she'd been punched in the stomach. Her eyes widened and she instantly went into self-defence mode, taking one step back, arms folded, although this time, unlike when her boss turned lascivious eyes on her, it was for an entirely different reason.

This time it was because the sudden bloom of sexual awareness shocked her.

She wanted to stare and just keep on staring. His black hair was slightly too long and swept back from a face that was chiselled to the sort of perfection no camera could ever fully capture. Midnight-dark eyes were fringed with lush dark lashes, his nose was aquiline and his mouth wide and crazily sensual. Every single thing about the man emanated the sort of fierce, aggressive sex appeal that made her heart beat a little faster and sent liquid heat pooling between her thighs, dampening her underwear.

It was an immediate reaction that infuriated her because Sofia *knew* that she should know better.

From the age of thirteen she had known what it felt like to be the unwilling object of attention from the opposite sex. She had fought off unwanted, uninvited advances and then, when she'd been fifteen, one advance in particular from a married friend of her mother's had made her realise that her looks weren't a blessing in disguise. They were a curse.

Since then, she had been at pains to guard herself against men, holding out for 'the one' but not caring all that much if 'the one' never came her way—just knowing that she would never, ever sell herself short or settle for anything less than what she thought she deserved.

And she would certainly never allow looks to define her the way they had her mother.

'You'd better come in,' she said, a little more

sharply than she'd intended. She stood back and the guy brushed past her. And there it went again…that tingle of sexual awareness that seemed to bypass all her natural defence systems.

She inched back when, having surveyed the impressive hall, he spun round to look at her.

'Where are they?'

'Who?'

'The Walters. Where are they? Shouldn't they be here to meet and greet?'

Sofia was torn between marvelling at the sheer audacity of the man and bristling at his arrogance.

He was looking at her, his dark eyes veiled and lazily assessing.

'I don't think they were planning on deferring their skiing holiday to give the temporary gardener the red-carpet treatment.'

'Nice house.'

'Is that all you've brought with you by way of luggage?' She eyed the battered hold-all.

Rafael shrugged. 'I like to travel light.'

'Can I get something for you to drink? Eat?'

'Is that your job here? Housekeeper?'

Rafael knew exactly what the woman did. In fact, he knew a great deal more about her than she ever could have imagined, because he had done some extensive background checks himself. His godfather might have had romantic notions of destiny throwing a daughter his way. Rafael was a little less trusting on that front.

The one thing he hadn't known was just quite how stunning she would be in the flesh. Long, dark, curling hair was carelessly tied back. Her skin was the colour of pale coffee and as smooth as silk and her eyes were vivid green, densely lashed and almond-shaped.

Not exactly the meek and mild goody-two-shoes his godfather was doubtless hoping for. Wasn't life full of surprises?

'I'm the nanny.' Sofia stuck out her chin at a defiant angle. She was a nanny, and she wasn't ashamed of that, but in her heart she could have been so much more. However, a chequered background that involved far too much moving around had wreaked havoc with her education.

Hopes for a rewarding career had died a slow death over the years, because doors never opened for someone with a patchy academic record. Yes, she was making up for lost time now, but it wasn't going to happen overnight, and meanwhile…

'Does the nanny have a name?'

'Sofia. Sofia Suarez. You never said—do you want anything to eat or drink? Naturally, I cannot raid the liquor cabinet to offer you anything alcoholic, but tea? Coffee? I could make you a sandwich.'

'Nothing alcoholic? In that case, I'll forgo the tea and coffee for some water, and a sandwich would be good.' He strolled through the kitchen. Big kitchen. Big house. Expensive people leading an expensive lifestyle.

'Please don't touch anything,' she said anxiously from behind him as he began opening drawers. Rafael slowly turned to look at her.

'If they've left you in charge here, they must expect you to open drawers and cupboards.'

'Of course, but…' Slow, hot colour crept into her cheeks.

'But you're the nanny and, when it comes to pecking order, the nanny ranks higher than the gardener?'

'You don't look like a gardener,' Sofia said,

changing the subject and turning her back to him as she expertly began making him a ham and cheese sandwich, which was exactly what she had had for her lunch. She hadn't yet had dinner but somehow breaking bread with this dark, arrogant man sent a trickle of cold apprehension racing up and down her spine.

Rafael grunted, watching and appreciating the length of her limbs, the willowy suppleness of her body, the innate grace with which she carried herself.

'You need to check her out,' his godfather had said urgently. 'I know I'm harbouring romantic notions of this young lady, but I'm no fool. I don't know what she's like, what sort of character she has. My dear boy, it would mean so much to me if you could check her out, but incognito. She must have no idea of the vast fortune that could be hers, as I wouldn't want that to influence her responses.

'To be blunt, I wouldn't want her to edit her personality to appeal. I would hope for someone kind, considerate, smart…and if she's not, well, a bridge to be crossed but not yet. Check her out—that's number one. And then…here's the sweetener to the deal if you take this on, my dear boy…my company. All my shares. You can move in and troubleshoot my stepson back into place. With my own flesh and blood in place, rightfully there, and you by her side at the helm, all my worries would end. You have said yourself that your own empire virtually runs itself. It's time you found a new challenge.'

Rafael had no need for his godfather's shares, although the leisure business would certainly be a healthy addition to his own vast portfolio. No, what motivated him went beyond anything tangible. The bottom line was that David had been there for him, mentor and friend, during all those long years when his own parents had jumped ship to do their own thing. His earliest memories of happiness didn't involve his parents. They involved his godfather. Without him, his life would have lacked all structure, and God only knew where he would have ended up. David was the only human being Rafael actually loved and there was no request he would ever have turned down. The handover of shares, which would enable him to sort out the problem with Freddy, was icing on the cake.

'Have you...um...?' Sofia found that she was flustered and distracted by the play of muscle and sinew just visible beneath the old T-shirt and faded jeans as he strolled to sit at the kitchen table, a vast affair fashioned out of glass and chrome and hideously unsuitable for anyone with kids.

'Have I...um...what?'

'Been a gardener for long,' Sofia said with strained politeness as her disobedient eyes fastened onto his lean, beautiful face, only to skitter away in alarm because she *never* stared at any man. It just wasn't her thing. Least of all an over-the-top-good-looking one like this because, in her experience, good-looking always signalled trouble.

Just like that, he looked up, their eyes tangled and for a few seconds she found that she couldn't breathe.

'It's a burgeoning career,' Rafael said vaguely. 'And, on the subject of people not looking the part, you look nothing like a nanny.'

Sofia stiffened, wondered whether this was going to be the start of the flirting game. He was going to be stationed in the annex by the pool. Coming as he did by word of mouth, she doubted that he would prove any kind of threat, but he could prove a nuisance, and she *was* going to be here on her own with him.

'Do you have a lot of experience of nannies?' she asked courteously. 'Maybe you expect me to be older? Perhaps with a wart or two on my chin?'

'We could have conversed in Spanish but I am more comfortable speaking English and you've answered in kind. You're bilingual. Not what I would have expected.' Rafael pushed away his empty plate and then relaxed back with his hands behind his head. 'Now that we're on the subject of expectations.'

'You're finished eating. I think I should show you where you'll be staying. Like you said, you're hot and tired.'

'Is that your way of telling me that you don't want me asking any more questions?'

Sofia shrugged and didn't bother to beat about the bush. 'I suppose it is.'

Rafael didn't budge. He was here on a mission. The sooner he got the job done, the quicker he would be able to dump this ridiculous charade of being a gardener. The closest he'd ever got to gardening was the book he'd bought the day before he left London. He'd speed-read a few pages. How hard could it be to turn over some soil and run a lawn mower over a lawn? But, still, he didn't want to hang around.

But first he had to get past whatever defences this woman had erected and suss her out.

More than that. If she passed the litmus test...

His dark eyes roved lazily over her. Graceful as a gazelle and just as skittish...

'What's it like, working here?' He chose to prolong the conversation.

Sofia clicked her tongue in annoyance. 'I thought you were tired. If I show you to your quarters, you can get an early night, and to-morrow I have a list of what you need to do.'

'I've never been a fan of early nights. What other languages do you speak?'

'What others do *you*?'

'French. Spanish. Italian. Some Mandarin. A sprinkling of a few others...'

'Very unusual for *a gardener*,' Sofia said tartly and Rafael laughed under his breath.

'*Touché.* I learnt them on the various jobs

I've had over the years. I also have a curious mind and, face it, if people are conversing in a foreign language around you then you need to understand what they're saying, as far as I am concerned. What about you?'

Sofia hesitated. She rarely got the chance to talk to guys. When she wasn't working, she was studying, looking ahead to a brighter future.

Guys and dating didn't feature in her calendar, not at this point in time.

But having this good-looking man here in the kitchen, asking her about herself…

She could feel her guard drop a little. The man was going to be around until James and Elizabeth returned with the kids and chances were that they would be thrown into each other's company frequently. Life would be easier if she opened up a little.

And he *was* so damned good-looking, so darkly, sinfully spectacular, and he didn't make her feel…*threatened*.

She was far too practical for a guy like him to get to her, but he was brilliant eye-candy, and it wouldn't hurt to give a little. At least *converse*.

'I… I spent a great deal of my life on the

move,' she volunteered hesitantly. She sat opposite him and propped her hand under her chin. 'My mother and I actually used to live in this part of the world, and we returned here eventually, but in the interim life was spent with suitcases at the ready.'

'That so? Why? It's a beautiful area…just the sort of place made for roots being put down.'

Sofia shrugged. There was only so far she was prepared to go sharing confidences with a complete stranger, however compelling his attentiveness was. 'At any rate, we moved about a bit, here and there. Long story, and frankly none of your business. I picked up English from some of the people we met along the way and made sure to practise whenever I could. I've always been good at languages.'

And libraries had such huge choice when it came to audio-learning. Wherever and whenever, she'd made the local library her first port of call. In a life of constant moving, libraries had become safe havens, places of stillness and peace. There was a big world out there and she would need to be fluent in English to navigate it successfully. One day.

'And your mother? Where is she now?'

Sofia glanced away. 'She died a few months ago. But she'd been ill for a couple of years prior to that. If it's all the same to you, I'd rather not talk about that.' She stood up and smiled politely. 'I'll show you where you'll be staying.'

Rafael vaulted upright. As he came to stand behind her, once again Sofia was intensely aware of his physicality.

At five-ten, she was tall, but he was several inches taller and something about his height, his muscularity, his lazy, masculine magnetism, made her feel feminine and girlish and nothing like the woman with her head firmly screwed on who was determined to control the outcome of her life because she had never had much control over the experiences of her past.

She'd moved from her home in Argentina to another and another before her mother had decided that settling down with an American tourist who had been backpacking through South America at the time might be a good idea. He had been ten years her junior and as responsible as a toddler. The marriage had lasted a year and a half, at which point he had disappeared back to his home in Florida, and they had upped sticks and headed in the opposite direction.

Story of her mother's life. Pregnant by an older man who had dumped her, breaking her heart in the process, from there on she had launched herself into a career of making the most of her good looks, which had never faded over time.

But that had all changed when, after years spent abroad, they had returned to her mother's home town where she had spent her final years being cared for by her sister, old friends who had rallied together and, of course, her daughter.

She wondered what this guy would make of her convoluted life history. He had landed here, roving gardener, so he must love moving around, never standing still, the very things she had come to loathe. They couldn't be more different and yet the urge to confide was so strong that it was scary.

'If you're ready?' She eyed his bag and moved towards the door. 'I have things to do...' She glanced away from dark, speculative eyes that were a little too interested for her liking.

So darkly, dangerously sexy…

For a fleeting second she wondered… *What is he really doing here…?*

CHAPTER TWO

'NICE PLACE,' RAFAEL said neutrally as they headed out of the house, swinging round to the back, away from the main lodgings.

Night had gathered around them and Rafael had morphed into a tall, dark shadow, his gait loose-limbed and oddly graceful for a man of his size.

Sofia was accustomed to the size of the mansion where she worked, as well as to the several acres of manicured lawns surrounding the house.

'It's very big,' she agreed, breathing in the fragranced air and making sure to keep some distance between them. It was cooler now, with a whispery breeze that lifted her hair and blew tendrils away from her face.

'Enjoy working here?'

'That's where you'll be staying. Straight

ahead. It's entirely self-contained, so there will be no need for you to come to the main house.'

'Unless I want to.'

Sofia shivered and hugged herself. She had picked up something in that low, lazy drawl but then, when she thought about it, she wondered whether it wasn't her imagination playing tricks on her.

'Have you been to this part of the world before?'

'This particular country has passed me by,' Rafael murmured.

'In that case, I can tell you where you need to go to buy…err…food or whatever else you might need.'

'Or you could show me.'

Sofia didn't say anything. Was this a come-on? It *sounded* like one but it didn't *feel* like one because his drawl was lazy and mildly amused. None of that skin-crawling invasion of her privacy and space that always alerted her to a man on the make.

She thought back to all those years ago and to one of those men on the make, but she had just been a kid of fifteen and he had been old enough to be her father—a friend of a friend of her mother's, drunk at a house party, one of the few her mother had ever had. She remembered the terror of her bedroom door slowly being pushed open and the fear when she had worked out why he had crept into the room.

Sofia knew that she might not have had the strength to fight him off and that he had only scarpered because a couple had stumbled up the stairs, opening doors in search of the upstairs bathroom. They had spooked the guy out of the bedroom because, drunk as he was, he'd still known what the fallout would be if he were to be caught. She'd been saved by the bell but it had been a sharp learning curve for her. *Be wary* had become the motto branded at the back of her brain, and she had lived her life accordingly.

Four years later, when she had made the mistake of falling for a boy her own age—only to discover that she had been the object of a bet as to whether he could get the hot chick into bed inside a month—'be wary' had become 'stay away'.

She was disturbed that these wayward memories had jumped out of her without warning because she'd always thought that they were buried and forgotten.

She slid her eyes sideways. He wasn't looking at her. He was frowning and staring at the grand quarters they were approaching, usually used as guest quarters for overspill at parties. James had decided that it would do for the gardener, possibly because it would have been unthinkable to accommodate him in the main house. A gardener roaming through their luxury villa and making himself at home in their kitchen would never have done.

Sofia stuck the key in the lock and stood back so that he could precede her into the two-bedroomed dwelling. She switched on all the lights and watched as he strolled around for a few seconds before heading off in the direction of the kitchen, having tossed his battered hold-all on the ground by the staircase.

She followed. The housekeeper had tidied the place but it felt stuffy and airless.

'Who usually uses this?' He appeared in the doorway of the kitchen and lounged indolently against the doorframe, looking at her with his head tilted to one side.

'Overnight guests. If the big house is full.' He was so breathtakingly beautiful that she couldn't help but stare at him. It was almost too much of a mammoth effort to look away.

'I'm surprised they didn't choose to stick you in here,' he mused, spinning around and then heading straight for the kitchen cupboards, which he proceeded to open and close. 'The very least they could have done was to equip me with a few essentials.'

Sofia gasped and then burst out laughing, surprising herself as much as it seemed to surprise Rafael. Laughing with a guy, any guy, wasn't something she could remember having done in years.

'Share the joke?' He raised both eyebrows and her outburst of laughter subsided into a wicked grin.

'You. You're so…so…*brazen*…'

'Explain.' But he was smiling crookedly back at her, his dark eyes unreadable.

'You don't seem at all grateful to be here.'

'Why should I be grateful?'

'Well, I gather from the Walters that they were more or less put in a position where they had to give you this gardening job for a month. It's a really cushy number.' She glanced around her at the luxurious accommodation. 'And most people would be over the moon to have this place to stay.'

'I'm not most people,' Rafael said. 'You'll figure that out soon enough.' He paused but kept his fabulous eyes pinned to her face, which made her colour rise further and made her heart flutter a little more furiously in her chest.

'Well, upstairs is self-explanatory. Two bedrooms and there's linen in the cupboard on the landing.'

'You still haven't told me why you don't stay out here.'

'I...the Walters... James and Elizabeth think it's more convenient for me to be at hand. You know...close to the kids.'

'Actually, I don't know.' He began heading up the stairs and for a few seconds Sofia wasn't sure whether he actually expected her to traipse along in his wake or not. She had shown him the lodge, she'd done what she had to do, and in the morning she would show him the list of stuff she had been given for him to start on. Elizabeth kept a vigilant eye on the garden but messages were always relayed via her husband to the team that came weekly to prune, trim, plant and uproot. He was officious in his dealings with them. He wouldn't be winning any popularity contests with his employees any time soon. He'd had no choice but to house this outrageous stranger but he had made sure to leave two A4 sheets of paper full of detailed instructions.

'What do you mean?' She roused herself from her ruminations and found herself following him up the stairs, stopping short as he pushed open one of the bedroom doors, before spinning around to look at her through narrowed eyes.

'I mean,' Rafael said slowly, 'By having you on tap, well, does that mean that you don't get any time off?'

'No, well...' Flustered, Sofia met his dark, speculative gaze, vibrant green eyes clashing with dark, fathomless ones. 'They do go out quite a bit and it's just more convenient for me to be there rather than having to decamp all the time when I need to babysit.'

'And do you get paid extra for all this babysitting? Hefty price for being on permanent stand by?'

'Why are you asking me all these questions?' she threw at him, uncomfortable because he was voicing the very resentments that had piled up inside her over the months. The job was extremely well paid but in return...

She needed the money. That was the bottom line. She had debts and nothing had been left when her mother had died. She had returned to ground zero after a long spell away with not much to show for it. One child, one divorce, any number of relationships that had ended up nowhere and only just enough money made over the years to ensure that her mother had enough for tickets back to base camp and sufficient cash as a down payment on a rented condo on the outskirts of Buenos Aires, close to where her sister lived.

Sofia had not had the opportunity to do any saving of her own and this nanny job was well paid—their luck with nannies hadn't been stellar, from what Elizabeth Walters had let slip, and Sofia wondered whether they'd set this sort of honey trap to ensure she wasn't tempted to quit.

'I'm a curious kind of guy,' Rafael said mildly, watching her carefully. So carefully that she began to fidget. 'Stay a while,' he coaxed, strolling out of the room, his demeanour that of lord rather than serf. He glanced over his shoulder as she followed like a puppet, which was not like her at all. 'I'm new to this country. I don't know a soul. It would be nice for me to have some company this evening, if only to learn a little about the place, so that I can familiarise myself better with it when I get out there to explore.'

'You're here to pull up weeds and plant shrubs, not explore,' Sofia reminded him, but she felt that tug of amusement again. He was so high-handed that it should have put her back up, but strangely it didn't.

Where she had spent her life trying hard to stay under the radar—partly to deter the advances of lecherous men and partly because she was so focused on her future that she knew that, at least for her, diplomacy was definitely the better part of valour—he was the opposite. Oil to her water, chalk to her cheese, darkness to her light.

She shivered, wondering whether the strange pull she felt tugging her towards him stemmed from the fascination she felt when confronted with her polar opposite or whether she wasn't just lonely.

Rafael shrugged. 'And I'm sure I'll be doing just that but I don't intend to come all the way out here and leave…empty-handed.'

'What does that mean?' Sofia questioned.

'It means that this is a beautiful part of the world and I won't be burying myself in somebody's back garden pulling up weeds without taking some time out to surface.'

'I don't think James Walters is going to appreciate your sense of adventure.'

Rafael shrugged.

'Don't you care?' Sofia asked curiously.

'Why should I?'

'Because you could end up with a poor reference. Mr Walters would enjoy nothing better.'

She blushed a bright red. 'Sorry. I shouldn't have said that.'

'But you did.' He began heading out of the lodge and back towards the main house, and Sofia was struck yet again by the man's arrogant assumption that he could do whatever he wanted, safe in the knowledge that no one was going to object. In this instance, the 'no one' just happened to be *her*. She'd already walked him to the lodge, and left him in no doubt that she wasn't interested in his company, yet he had decided to ignore her completely. She belatedly remembered how keen she had been to be rid of him and how annoyed she'd been at his late arrival.

'You don't like the man, do you?' he remarked casually without looking around, throwing it over his shoulder as an aside.

'I never said that!'

'I'm good at reading what people choose not to say. In fact...' He stopped dead in his tracks and stared down at her thoughtfully. 'I'd say a person can learn more about someone from what they choose to keep secret. If you don't like working for these people, then why do you?'

'Why do you think?' Sofia asked tartly. 'For the same reason you're here! The money. Look, don't you have stuff to do? Unpack? Touch base with your friends and relatives to tell them that you've arrived safe and sound?'

'I don't have much to unpack and notifying friends and relatives can wait. I'll have that cup of coffee you offered earlier. If you feel guilty about doing something in the big house that doesn't involve working for them and obeying orders even when they're not around, then you can fill in some time by telling me what they want me to do around here. Although I'm sure there's a helpful list as long as my arm.'

'One coffee…'

'I get it. Then you have things to do.'

This time, he spent a bit longer inspecting the house as they entered. He pushed open doors while Sofia watched, knowing that she should say something but not sure what, because she didn't think he was going to make off with the family silver.

The guy was dressed in clean but worn

clothes, but something about him, some in-stinct, told her that he was no thief and that he saw nothing wrong with checking out his sur-roundings.

She wondered whether his bone-deep con-fidence was born from the fact that he was so spectacularly good-looking, but then she thought about herself and the way her looks had the opposite effect on her, making her timid, cautious and always ready to bolt. Maybe when it came to the lottery of good looks it was dif-ferent for guys—she didn't imagine that Rafael would have been hounded by jealous peers and plagued by the wandering hands of women he didn't want near him, fearful that they might take advantage.

She just knew that he sent shivers of aware-ness racing up and down her spine.

She made them both a mug of coffee and, because she was hungry again, she fixed her-self something to eat, another sandwich, while he looked on, his dark eyes watching her with veiled, lazy interest.

'Is it because you like kids?'

'I beg your pardon?'

'The reason why you're here, working for a couple you don't respect.'

'You're jumping to all sorts of conclusions!'

'Am I?'

'I'm not asking *you* a load of questions.'

'What would you like to know?' Rafael murmured softly, leaning back into his chair and angling it so that he could hook his foot under another and scrape it towards him to use it as a footrest.

He folded his hands behind his head and stared at her.

'How did you manage to wangle the job here?'

'I have a few connections. Does it matter?'

'I don't suppose so…'

'You never answered my question about whether you worked here because you liked kids. Do you have any siblings?' Again, another question. Rafael already knew the answer but he had been tasked with finding out about the woman, and he intended to do so just whatever way he chose. An evasion here…a little white lie there…so many things could unlock the secret of a person's personality, and when a fortune was at stake unlocking her personality was more than just a technicality.

'No.' Sofia hesitated and her cut-glass green eyes clouded over. 'I'm an only child. My mother…fell in love with some old guy when she was in her twenties.'

'Some old guy?'

'Well, my father, as it happens, who was much older than her.' Sofia grimaced. 'She didn't like talking about it. In fact, she didn't for most of my life, but then when she got ill she began opening up a bit more…'

Rafael was watching her carefully. 'So where is he now?'

'Who knows? It didn't last.'

'Why not?'

'It doesn't matter. It ended because that's the way most relationships go. They end.'

'You're very jaded for someone as young as you are. Why? And did you ever want to find out about…the old guy?'

'Why should I?' Her eyes flashed sudden, blazing anger.

Rafael shrugged. 'Curiosity?'

'I'm too busy trying to get on with living my

life to be curious about anyone or anything,' Sofia muttered.

'That's a lie.'

'What?'

'You're lying. You're curious about me. I can see it on your face and hear it in your voice.'

'You're incredibly egotistic!'

'I'm curious about you as well. You're not travelling down a one-way street, Sofia…'

The suddenly charged silence that followed his remark stretched and stretched to breaking point. Rafael vaulted fluidly upright and proceeded to prowl through the kitchen, then he disappeared into the adjoining pantry to reappear with a bottle of wine. He raised both eyebrows at her horrified expression. 'I'm sure your dictator employers won't mind if we crack open this bottle of wine to make the time go quicker.'

'You can't!' She released a long breath, confused and addled.

'Are you going to stop me?' He hunted down a corkscrew and a couple of crystal glasses and poured. He held out the glass and, after a moment's hesitation, Sofia took it.

They hadn't exactly locked the wine away but she'd known, without having to be told, that all alcohol was off-limits for her. She had never had a problem with that because she wasn't much of a drinker, and she respected the boundaries they had laid down.

But that rebellious streak she hadn't even known existed sparked into life again, filling her with a sense of wicked daring as she sipped some of the red wine.

'Don't worry,' Rafael murmured, swirling his glass and breathing in the fragrant aroma for a few seconds, appreciating the quality of the grape. 'I'll make sure I replace it.'

'If you plan on drinking any more of this stuff,' Sofia grimaced, 'Then you're going to find that you've blown all your earnings before you've even done a day's work in the garden! The Walters are very fussy when it comes to their wines. I have no idea how much this bottle cost but it won't be cheap.'

'Which is why you're terrified of going near that wine fridge?'

'Drinking isn't appropriate when you're looking after children.'

'And, as you've said, you're on call twenty-four hours a day, every day of the week...' He strolled towards the huge double-fronted steel grey fridge and stared at drawings that had been attached by magnets to the front, oddly out of place in the vast, modern, clinically pristine surroundings. He un-tacked a photo and peered at it, then he looked at her.

'This the family?' He tilted his head to one side and Sofia knew that she was reddening. Her skin felt hot and prickly and there was a throbbing in her temples. Those dark, dark eyes of his were so intense, so *penetrating*.

'Yes,' she replied shortly.

'Attractive couple. Attractive kids.'

'Yes. They are.'

'Younger than I'd imagined, if I'm honest.'

'Why would you have imagined anything about them?'

'Unlike you, I don't pretend to be incurious. It's natural to wonder about the sort of people you might be stuck with for a couple of weeks.'

'You act as though *you're* doing *them* a favour!'

'The man...is very good-looking, wouldn't

you agree?' Rafael murmured, glancing towards her, keeping his keen gaze pinned to her face.

Sofia tensed, her face tight, and just like that he replaced the photo from where it had been taken, seemingly losing all interest in the conversation.

In *her.*

Disappointment warred with relief. She looked at the glass of wine in her hand and wondered how she'd ended up straying from the straight and narrow.

'So what's keeping you here?' he asked. 'Aside from two kids and a pay packet at the end of the month.'

The question temporarily threw her and she looked at him with sudden bewilderment.

'Isn't that enough? We all have to earn a living. You're here, earning a living.' She cleared her throat, finished her wine and stood up, hot, bothered and so, so conscious of his eyes trained on her face. 'Anyway, you should… be thinking about heading back to your lodge. You'll be busy tomorrow.' She stood up while he remained sitting where he was, long legs stretched out in front of him, lightly holding his glass of wine and idly twirling it before taking a sip.

'Sit, why don't you?' He motioned to the chair and drawled with a ghost of a wry smile, 'I promise that I'll leave you in peace when this glass of wine is finished.'

Sofia thought of the empty evening stretching ahead of her and was ashamed to find herself wanting him to hang around. She'd always enjoyed her own company, especially since she'd been working here, because her time was so seldom her own. However, he'd sparked a curious restlessness inside her and the prospect of studying, which had been top of the agenda, seemed dull and boring.

Disobedient eyes slid across to him, to the lazy, 'Lord of the Manor' way he sat there, sprawled in the kitchen chair, dominating the space around him.

Fearless. What sort of gardener was he anyway?

She tried to picture him weeding, scrutinising bottles of fertiliser, mowing the lawn and talking to the plants but she couldn't.

'Is there someone significant lurking in the background, making all this drudgery worthwhile? He must be very understanding to put up with you being on call twenty-four-seven.'

'Drudgery? *Drudgery?* Who do you think you are?'

'Figure of speech,' Rafael said unapologetically.

'I *resent* that figure of speech!'

'You're very attractive but I don't suppose I'm telling you anything you don't already know.'

'That doesn't mean...it *doesn't mean...*' She was breathless and had to breathe in deeply to stop herself from shaking. 'That there's a significant *anyone lurking in the background*, and even if there was I fail to see what business it might be of *yours*!'

Rafael didn't say anything for a few seconds and she found the silence oppressive, like a dense weight pushing down on her, making her want to justify herself.

She thought of her experiences with the opposite sex, the hungry eyes and groping hands that she had always had to bat away. She thought of being the object of a bet, mortified and humiliated at a time when she had been so open to handing over her heart to someone.

Was it any wonder that she felt safest when she was buried behind books, studying and dreaming about an uncomplicated future?

Other girls her age dreamt of guys, dating, engagements and getting married.

She dreamt of being able to take care of herself. When she thought about men, she vaguely had in her head someone unthreatening—dull, even. Someone who would be able to see past the sexy image that was so unlike the girl she was inside and appreciate her for the qualities that weren't on show.

'So no boyfriend?'

'No,' she said sharply. 'Not that it's any of your business.' She abruptly got to her feet and made a beeline for the folder she had been given with all the detailed instructions for the gardener whom had been foisted upon the Walters.

'And what about the master of the house?' Rafael quizzed softly, feeling her out.

Sofia stiffened. It was barely noticeable but *he* noticed it.

'What,' Sofia asked coldly, 'are you implying?'

'Sometimes masters of the house can have expectations beyond the call of duty. Sometimes those expectations are met...'

Sofia clenched her fists and took a deep, steadying breath, which didn't do the trick. He was being provocative. She had no idea why but it wasn't going to get her anywhere if she allowed her temper to get the better of her. Letting your emotions get the better of you never paid off. Her mother had let her emotions get the better of her. First when she had fallen for a guy who had dumped her, and afterwards when she had let her heart rule her head, always looking for salvation in someone else, always thinking that she could escape disappointment by throwing herself headlong into relationships that had never gone anywhere.

Sofia had adored her fallible mother but had seen the failings and had determined never to be afflicted in the same way.

Letting this complete stranger get to her wasn't going to work.

'Not in this case,' she said through gritted teeth.

'I didn't think so,' Rafael murmured honestly. 'But there's something there, isn't there? What?'

'Let's get something straight.' Sofia was holding on to her temper with difficulty and he wasn't making it any easier by that all-knowing look on his face, a look which implied that he could read her mind, which of course he couldn't.

'What's that?'

'You're here to do a job. I have stuff to do and I won't be fraternising with you.'

'Because I ask too many questions?'

'My personal life is none of your business. Now, I'll show you to the door. Take the instructions. You might want to read them over before you go to bed. There will be a lot to busy yourself with until James and Elizabeth get back. They'll expect you to have done everything laid out, right down to pulling up the very last weed in the flower beds.' She thrust the paper into his hand, and he glanced at it as though only really mildly curious as to the content.

'Later.'

'Later? *Later?*'

Rafael rose to his feet unhurriedly. 'I'll be settling in before I start doing any work in someone's garden.'

'Settling in?' she parroted, staggered and still seething at his outrageous implications. For all that, though, she was furiously aware of the keen beating of her heart and the way, for the first time in living memory, she felt *alive* to someone else, all her senses heightened, her pulses racing, her skin tingling.

Rafael burst out laughing. 'Oh yes,' he said in a low, velvety undertone, moving towards the door and dumping the unopened pages of instructions on the kitchen counter *en route*. 'I intend to familiarise myself with the place before I go anywhere near a bottle of weed killer or a lawn mower.'

'You can't do that.'

'Will you be trying to stop me?'

'James… Mr Walters…he can be very short-tempered.'

'Really?'

Sofia nodded, but she was mesmerised by the arrogant lack of interest in Rafael's dark gaze.

'Interesting.'

'What is?' she breathed, hovering, unable to keep still.

'Interesting how incredibly unadventurous you are for someone of your age. Why is that? No, I can guess why. Your mother dragged you from pillar to post and your response was to batten down the hatches and pray for a time when the storm would pass.'

'Stop,' Sofia hissed, shaken. 'Stop making assumptions about my personal life!'

Rafael didn't say anything for a few seconds but he looked at her, a long, leisurely look that made her breath hitch in her throat.

'A little adventure can go a long way,' Rafael murmured.

'Maybe for you,' she was stung into responding, 'but not for me. So maybe you're right— maybe a life of never quite staying anywhere long enough to put down real roots has made me a bit wary when it comes to all that nonsense about *adventure*. But I don't need a complete stranger to start lecturing to me on my life choices.'

'Who better than a complete stranger to lecture on life choices? Isn't that how therapy works?'

'You're a gardener, not a therapist, so I'm not seeing the relevance.'

Rafael adroitly swerved around the interruption. 'Life is meant to be lived,' he mused, eyes pinned to her face, noting every change of expression, every fleeting shadow, the flare of her nostrils, the dilation of her pupils, the way her breathing was shallow and breathless. 'Sometimes, things happen that can't be predicted...' He shrugged and grinned. 'All I'm saying is that I won't be spending every hour of the day obeying what's on those pieces of paper *el señor de la casa* has thoughtfully printed for me.'

Adventure...

Never before had one word dangled before her eyes, beckoning with the seductive allure of a banquet spread before a starving person.

She had made all the right noises about adventure being the last thing she wanted in her life. She'd meant every word of it! It was an ideology long ingrained inside her.

And yet...he stood there and the urge to be

swept away by that low, sexy voice was over-whelming. She physically had to take a step back but her heart was beating like a sledge-hammer inside her.

'I intend to see a bit of this beautiful place, Sofia, and you're going to be my guide,' he murmured. 'While the cat's away the mouse, I'm suggesting, should definitely play...'

CHAPTER THREE

SOFIA EYED THE crystal-clear swimming pool with a mixture of headiness and apprehension.

Under a dazzlingly bright-blue sky, the flat turquoise water glittered and shimmered and beckoned on a day of soaring temperatures.

Of course, she'd used the pool before, but only when the children had been around, splashing and yelling, with the little one clinging to her while she did her best to make sure Josh wasn't going to do himself permanent damage by flinging himself into the water from the side of the pool while helping his younger sister to keep afloat without arm bands.

This time round...

Sofia closed her eyes and took a few steadying breaths while she mentally confronted the position she now found herself in.

'Out of her comfort zone' summed it up.

More than *out*, she thought giddily. More like

teetering on the edge of a precipice with the comfort zone no longer in sight.

Amazing what a week could do!

First of all, she had let herself be talked into a sightseeing tour of Buenos Aires.

'Live a little,' he had whispered in a dangerously soft voice and even more dangerous glint in his dark eyes.

Then, in quick succession, there had followed various little jaunts in and around the city, while she had relaxed more and more and found herself dropping her guard and laughing, her curiosity about the stranger who had landed on the Walters' doorstep growing with each passing second.

A stranger who had not bothered to go near the long list of must-dos that her employer had meticulously and maliciously printed off.

A stranger who had not, in fact, been near the tool shed, the ride-on mower, the green house or any implement connected to gardening.

His audacity thrilled her.

She wasn't going to lose her head, because he wasn't 'settling down' material, and he would be gone in the blink of an eye. But where was the harm in *having a bit of fun*, as he had cleverly suggested to her?

And she *was* having fun. Lots of it.

Even her aunt had noticed.

The evening before, she had gone to visit Misa, who lived on the other side of the city where the tall, shiny towers of the city and the exclusive retreats of the wealthy were as out of reach as the moon—even though, from the bedroom window of the derelict house in which she lived, Misa could spy them in the distance.

'You're glowing,' her aunt had announced, pleased. 'It's the first time you've actually looked like a young girl since you returned to Buenos Aires. There must be a man in your life. Someone special, Sofia?'

'I'm not glowing,' Sofia had protested, but she knew that she was somehow *different*.

She had hardly been able to focus on Miguel, her cousin, who as always was in his room, immobile and frustrated, facing certain physical disabilities after a motorcycle accident at the age of sixteen.

For once, instead of sitting back and listening to his despair, Sofia had talked about the stranger who had landed on the doorstep like a breath of fresh air.

She'd been full of it.

Her head had been giddy with thoughts of Rafael when she'd left, whereas normally she would be in her usual funk, thinking about her aunt and Miguel stuck in one of the poorer *barrios* where block upon block of unsightly apartments jostled against one another like little card houses, unsubstantial and ready to topple over into the chaotic, cluttered little streets below. Thinking, as she always did, of how much Misa had been there for her much younger sister when Maria had returned ill and with time no longer on her side. Thinking of how vital was the money she earned as a nanny when it came to helping them both.

Now, with her towel in one hand, clad in the only swimsuit she possessed—an extremely unadventurous black one-piece—Sofia waited with shameful eagerness for Rafael to appear.

He had gone to the city 'to see what was going on' as though, somehow, people in high places might be clamouring for his involvement.

'But meet me at the pool,' he'd said in that

way he had of voicing the daringly unaccept-able as though she would be an idiot not to con-cede. 'I'll bring lunch.'

'You don't have to do that,' Sofia had laughed, captivated by the intensity of his gaze. 'Save what money you have! James and Elizabeth have left sufficient food in the larder for me to rustle something up.'

But he would have none of it and now here she was, waiting for him to appear with food, generous to a fault even though he was no higher up the pecking order than was she.

Her head was filled with dangerous, exciting possibilities.

He'd been the perfect gentleman so far, al-though his manner was amused, flirtatious, *sexy*, and his dark eyes lazily, thrillingly spec-ulative. She wasn't sure whether he fancied her or not and that was a first.

Lust was only something she'd read about in magazine articles but now...

Now it was something that called to her, the ultimate adventure waiting to happen. When she thought about being the one to make the first move, her whole body burned and tingled, but more and more in the space of a handful of days she had been contemplating just that.

She wasn't entirely sure about the technicalities of such an event, but she was willing to give it a go, and that was such alien territory for her that her nervous system went into meltdown when she thought about it.

Her head was in the clouds when she became aware of Rafael, who had paused just by the pool, face shadowed by the overhang of the tree he was standing beneath.

Her eyes roamed appreciatively over him. So tall, so powerfully built, so commanding. He was in a pair of low-slung, khaki shorts, a T-shirt that originally would have been black but was now an off-grey, and a pair of loafers that looked as though they cost the earth but which, Sofia knew, would have been as cheap as chips.

Something about the way he was put together made everything he wore look stupidly expensive.

She began walking towards him and her heart beat just a little faster, the closer she got.

He didn't move a muscle.

It was curious but there was something about him that was as wary as she was, even though he was crazily sexy and extremely forthcoming with conversation, able to reduce her to hysterics in just a few witty sentences, or have her hanging on his every word with anecdotes that beggared belief.

She was vaguely aware that there was a part of him that was very contained, so automatically she had responded like for like, confiding but only just so much, never letting him get too close.

He knew a lot about her experiences of travelling around with her mother but nothing at all about her life here, when she had finally returned to her home town.

He had guessed, shrewdly, at her experiences of being a nanny and working for James, but she had wisely held back from saying anything that could jeopardise the job which she badly needed, at least for the time being.

She had become close enough to *want* him in a very, very physical way, but had remained distant enough to protect herself, conscious of the temporary nature of his visit and the un-suitability of his personality.

'Hi.' She smiled and stared up at him, un-easily aware that he wasn't smiling back with his usual easy charm. 'I wondered whether you'd become lost in the city!' She chatted away, keeping some distance between them and wishing she had covered herself a little more, because the unreadable remoteness of his expression was making her feel vulnerable and exposed.

'Is it possible to become lost anywhere in the world if you're in possession of a smart phone?' he murmured.

'So true.' The smile was still there. 'Have you brought lunch? I'm ravenous.'

'Didn't have time in the end.' He raked his fingers through his hair and shifted on his feet before settling his dark eyes on her face. 'Sofia, we need to talk.'

'Sure.' The smile faltered and her defences slammed into place, and she stepped back, shielding her eyes to look up at him. 'I expect you've finally got round to realising that the Walters are going to be back pretty soon and you have to get down to actually doing some gardening.'

'I'd forgotten their existence, in point of fact. So, no, that realisation hasn't come home to roost.'

'Shall I make us something to eat? Er…we could talk in the kitchen. Or out here. Although, it's really hot, and anyway I shouldn't really be swimming in this pool. It's not what I'm being paid to do while my employers are away.'

'Going inside might be a good idea, Sofia. You're going to have to sit down to hear me out.'

'Really?' Her voice cooled because she could smell a warning a mile off. Had he noticed the way she had gradually thawed? Maybe he'd sensed her increasing desire and was politely about to tell her that he wasn't up for grabs.

She had no idea whether he was involved with anyone, or even married! She'd made assumptions and was now mortified that she might have got those assumptions wrong.

'Really.'

Rafael began walking towards the sprawling villa, and after a few seconds of hesitation Sofia followed in his wake.

He didn't swerve towards the kitchen. Instead, he headed towards the sitting room and then turned, waiting as she entered and then stopped dead in her tracks, hovering just inside the door.

'What's going on, Rafael?'

'Sit.'

'Thanks, but I'm fine standing right here.'

'I'm not entirely sure where to begin.' He paused. 'Maybe you should just take a look at this.' He flicked open his wallet and pulled out an article on his godfather that he had printed off before he had left London, knowing that when the story emerged the online entry might explain more than he would be able to. He handed her the paper and then stepped back to watch her face as she scanned it before returning it to him.

'So?' she flung challengingly at him.

'Recognise the name?'

'I haven't got a clue who that person is.'

'You mother never mentioned names when she was talking about your father?'

Colour leeched out of her face as she stared at him wordlessly for a few seconds. 'No.'

'The man you've just read about is your father.'

'I don't believe you.' She stumbled into the room and fell into one of the chairs, then promptly sat forward, horribly conscious of her state of undress. Primly, she draped the towel she had been carrying across her thighs and watched as he drew a chair to sit directly facing her.

Was this some sort of interrogation? Surely he couldn't be right? She tried frantically to remember what her mother had said about her father aside from, in her last few days, when she had repeatedly told her that he had broken her heart. Had she described the guy at all? No. He'd been much older than her at the time, but she had shied away from details. Sofia had never bothered to pry, because what would have been the use?

'Why wouldn't you? What reason would I have to lie?'

'Look, I don't know what's going on but—'

'Hear me out, Sofia, and you will. David

Dunmore is your father. Your mother contacted him shortly before she died. Her conscience, it would seem, got the better of her. She told him that he had a daughter. You. He had people check you out as soon as he received that letter from your mother.'

'Had people *check me out*?'

'These things happen.' Rafael shrugged.

'No. Not in my world, they don't happen.' She stared at him stonily. 'Who *are* you?' she demanded, leaping to her feet. 'I don't want to be having this conversation. I need to... I need to...'

'You need to sit and listen to what I have to say. Sofia, I didn't come over here from London to play at being a gardener.'

'Then why have you come?' She sat back down, very slowly, riveted to his beautiful face, chilled by the cold containment of his expression. This was certainly not the warm, teasing guy she had begun losing her head over. This was a stranger on a mission and it was dawning on her that the mission might not be to her liking.

But confusion rendered her speechless while

her thoughts buzzed in her head like a swarm of angry wasps.

'David Dunmore is my godfather and I was tasked with coming over here to personally check you out. Not check out the veracity of your identity, but to check out what sort of person you are.'

Sofia stared at him sickly as pieces of the jigsaw puzzle began meshing together, revealing a picture she didn't want to acknowledge.

'There must be some mistake,' she whispered. 'And even if there isn't…even if that *man* happens to be my father…why would he send someone over here to check and *see what I might be like*?'

'That *man* happens to be an extremely wealthy person,' Rafael told her flatly. 'Wealthy people take the necessary precautions.'

'And you…? If you're not a gardener, are *you* wealthy as well?'

'I am beyond wealthy.'

That statement of fact dimly registered in a part of her brain that was already recognising that this was no joke. This man—the man she'd thought she was getting to know, the one man to have broken through her defences—was not the person she had thought him to be. In short, he was a spy sent over to get the measure of her for reasons he hadn't fully disclosed, but which he was about to.

'I should have guessed,' she said bitterly.

'How so?'

'Just the way you were. Arrogant. Dismissive. How did you manage to wangle a job here as a gardener?'

'David managed that feat and, believe me, I was dubious about the validity of this…fishing expedition but…' He paused, expression thoughtful as he mulled over the direction the conversation should take.

Sofia watched. What else could she do? Watched, and waited and cursed herself for letting her trusted instinct to keep all men at arm's length go to pot.

She should have known that all that charm, those sinful good looks, that mesmerising personality came at a price. She was paying the price now as she accepted how far she had been sucked into the magical aura he exuded.

She'd been ready to fall into his arms and sleep with him!

'But…?' she questioned coldly.

'But, firstly, I should explain that he has no other natural children of his own. He's been married twice, and both marriages ended in divorce, and extremely acrimonious divorce at that. And neither of those marriages yielded any children, although he did inherit a stepson who now owns a substantial amount of shares in his company.'

'What does that have to do with me?'

'Ostensibly, it should have nothing to do with you whatsoever, but in point of fact you, by virtue of your blood line, are in line to naturally inherit the rest of the shares held by your father.'

'I have no idea where you're going with this.'

'Surely you're beginning to join the dots, Sofia?'

'Why would someone I've never met, someone who never knew I existed until a handful of months ago, care one way or another about blood lines?' She laughed scornfully.

'David's stepson,' Rafael informed her heavily, 'has been proving to be something of a problem ever since he came of age.' Rafael lapsed into temporary silence, his dark brows knitted in a frown. Without warning, he vaulted upright and began pacing the room, a vision of such superb grace and elegance that the breath caught in her throat and she had to look away to stop the treacherous pounding of her heart.

He came to rest directly in front of her, staring down into her upturned face.

'He was given shares courtesy of my godfather's extremely cunning ex-wife and her very efficient divorce lawyer. Not enough to take over the company but enough to be a nuisance. Under normal circumstances, David would be able to contain the situation, as he has done in the past, but his health has not been good.' Rafael's face shadowed. 'He has lost the desire and no longer has the energy to exert some much-needed control.'

'I still have no idea where you're going with this.'

'I was sent here to see whether you were a worthy heir.'

Silence settled between them. She looked

away, sick to her stomach, because she knew now that all that flirting, those dangerously seductive glances, that lazy banter that had made her squirm with crazy, stupid excitement and lust, had all been part of a bigger plan. While she'd been busy letting her heart rule her head, he'd been busy keeping tabs to see what sort of person she was.

'A worthy heir,' she said woodenly. 'A worthy heir to do what, exactly? Bond with someone I don't know from Adam and have no desire to meet?'

'A worthy heir to take over from David…at the very least in name.' He resumed sitting but this time there was a tension in his posture that hadn't been there before.

Sofia noted it without even realising that she was doing so. Her mind was too full of other things to pay attention to what was happening on the periphery of her consciousness.

She burst out laughing, genuine, unrestrained laughter, because the whole situation was beginning to feel a little preposterous. If it weren't for the deadly serious expression on Rafael's face, she would almost have expected a camera crew to jump out from behind the sofa, yelling that she'd been tricked.

'Share the joke?' Rafael asked coolly.

'What's funny is the thought of me being checked out to see if I fit the bill as a company director! I hate to break the bad news, but nannies don't really have that level of experience. Sure, I'm doing my accountancy exams in my own time, but somehow I don't think that's going to be sufficient, do you?'

'No. You could no more run my godfather's company than you could harness a horse and ride to the moon.'

'Thanks for the vote of confidence, Rafael,' Sofia said acidly.

'I'm being realistic. You're not equipped to go near a billion-dollar business. But here's where it gets interesting, Sofia.' His eyes locked to hers and a shiver ran up and down her spine, a fast, cold, tickling sensation that suddenly made her pulses race. 'I'm not just here to check your suitability as an heir. I'm here to check your suitability as a wife.'

For a few seconds she thought that she had misheard him. Her mouth fell open, her eyes widened, but whatever she wanted to stay remained stuck firmly in her throat.

'You're in shock,' Rafael told her calmly. He stood up, vanished for a couple of minutes while she remained sitting as frozen as a statue, then returned with a glass of something strong and golden and told her to drink it.

She obeyed and the fiery liquid coursed a burning path down her throat. It did the trick. She felt the tension ease out of her as she dared to meet his opaque, speculative gaze.

'Before you tell me that you may have heard incorrectly, let me assure you that you haven't. Not only was I asked to search you out and verify your personality, but dangling at the end of the request was a very tempting titbit. I marry you and I get ownership of vital sections of my godfather's companies. Vital shares in certain areas would remain within your control. It's complicated, because of the size of the concern, but suffice to say that David's proposition…' Rafael half-smiled, the tension draining away for a few seconds, 'Was pretty shrewd. The leisure side of his portfolio would be signed over to me, and that sly old fox has known for a long time that I've expressed interest in that side of his company, so handing it over would be quite the temptation. And, as your husband, I would legitimately be able to put things in order within the rest of the company and sort Freddy out once and for all.'

And his godfather would be happy. David's happiness was all that mattered to Rafael and, as far as he was concerned, a marriage of convenience unsullied by emotion made a lot of sense.

'You've got to be joking.'

'I fully intended to take a bit more time getting to know you, but I've broached this now because things have unexpectedly come to a head. My godfather...' He glanced away and Sofia saw the giveaway tightening of his jaw that revealed a depth of emotion that she suspected was never allowed to surface. 'My godfather, *your father*,' he continued, gathering himself in record time, 'has been rushed to the hospital with another heart attack. The consultant called me to say that he's out of surgery but whether he will fully recover or not remains to be seen.'

'I'm really sorry, Rafael.' Her natural instinct to empathise won over the horror of being manipulated by the man sitting in front of her.

'Let's leave that to one side,' was his brusque response. 'The fact is that time is no longer on my side. I came here to do a job—suss you out and take the necessary steps.'

'Well, you've wasted your time.' She stood up, empathy safely back in its box, and walked towards the door. She half-expected him to tell her to sit back down, but he didn't. However, she still didn't leave the room, as her head was telling her to do.

'Like I said, I don't know my father and I have no interest in finding out about him. And marry you?' She laughed incredulously. 'You're living on a different planet if you think that I would just walk up the aisle with some guy I've known for five minutes because he's running an errand for his godfather and I happen to be part of the errand!' When he didn't reply, she threw him a genuinely perplexed look, her slanting green eyes narrowed and questioning. 'And why would *you* consider marrying a perfect stranger anyway?'

'I see it as a business arrangement. I have no sentimental attachment to the notion of marriage. In fact, I'd never considered getting married at all until my godfather mentioned it. As arrangements go, it happened to be one that suited me on a number of fronts. It would solve the difficulties that have been plaguing my godfather for a while. I could legitimately go in and take control. And, like I said, it would also be a nice and interesting addition to my own portfolio of companies.'

'Why doesn't he just give you the whole damn lot and be done with it?'

'Perhaps he would have in time. Under normal circumstances, he wouldn't have considered it because he has always been a very vital man, more than capable of steering his vast company. But he's been diminished and Freddy has jumped into that breach to exploit it. Hence his proposal to me,' Rafael said honestly. 'And there's a great deal of sentimentality attached to seeing you. He would like to get to know the daughter he's never known…at any rate, that's my interpretation of events.'

'Not going to happen.' Sofia thought of the

way her mother's life had meandered in all sorts of unfortunate directions after that life-changing affair had ended, after she'd been dumped—no doubt because at the time David Dunmore had wanted nothing permanent with some woman who had been cleaning his room.

From remarks made over the years, confidences uttered when her mother had been dying, Sofia had worked out that her mother had fallen, and fallen hard, for a guy who had walked away from her, disappeared without warning and without a backward glance. Thereafter she had lost her innocent belief in all that nonsense about love conquering all. One minute he'd been there, hot in pursuit and spinning her stories about everlasting happiness, and then *poof*, he'd gone. She'd been told by his friend and colleague that he wouldn't be returning, that the best bet would be for her to hand in her notice and save herself the embarrassment of fingers pointing, because the whole messy business would hit the public domain sooner or later and she'd be kicked out.

Sofia had grown up with a mother who had traded her looks for promises of love, always searching for what she had lost and believing that she could recapture it. Loving the wrong guy had made her vulnerable. It was an excellent lesson when it came to choosing right.

'Because you have romantic dreams about what a marriage should be?' he questioned, expression unreadable.

Sofia stiffened and looked at him. She'd always thought herself far too practical to get swept up in the whole starry-eyed business of romance. She'd never wanted to be vulnerable the way her mother had been. Her head was firmly screwed on, and she liked it that way, but when she considered the past few days she had to admit to herself that silly romantic feelings had crept to the surface, altering the way she behaved, turning her into someone she didn't recognise.

All that for a guy who had been sent over to do a job and had probably figured that turning on the charm would be the most efficient way of succeeding in his task.

It was humiliating but she had to concede that a very wealthy, drop-dead sexy guy could have his pick of women and, even though she knew what it was like to turn heads, she was certainly not the most beautiful woman in the world.

'You could have anyone...' she heard herself say out loud and then blushed furiously at the lapse in concentration.

Rafael slowly smiled and tilted his head to one side. 'I could...' he agreed softly, without an ounce of false modesty. 'But I find that the price tag attached to getting too involved with a woman is one I'm not prepared to pay. My godfather is fully aware of my views on marriage, which is why he never thought twice about the offer he made. You may not want to get to know your father,' he continued, voice hardening, 'but, believe me, it would be very much worth your while.'

'I'm not a pawn on a chessboard to be pushed and manipulated.' She tilted her chin at a mutinous angle. He was so still, so focused, so beautiful.

It was an effort not to take a few steps closer, just to breathe him in and wallow in the impact on her senses.

It was insane. She had no idea how he had

managed to have that effect on her, but he had, and she hated her own weakness, especially now that she was finding out just what he was all about.

'Proud words,' Rafael murmured, moving towards her, taking his time, eyes darkening in unwitting appreciation. He was powerfully drawn to her even as his head warned against muddying the waters with unnecessary complications. 'I admire that, but you should really think about what's on offer here.'

'I've thought.'

'No, Sofia, you really haven't.' He looked around him, taking in the handsome proportions of the room, and then focused his fabulous eyes on her.

The effect was to render her breathless and confused.

'You see this as your future?'

'Of course I don't! I told you... I'm in the process of doing my accountancy exams...'

'Which won't be completed for...how long? Six months? A year? Longer? And in the meantime you remain here, working for some guy who wants to get his hands on you?'

'I never said anything of the sort!'

'You didn't have to.' He walked away from her, headed towards the window ledge, against which he perched with a magnificent sense of complete authority. 'Like I told you, I'm an expert when it comes to working out what's not being told.'

Addled and furious, Sofia thought of James and that way he had of looking at her, undressing her with his eyes. He would never do anything, because he was fearful of consequences, but he certainly didn't make life comfortable for her…and who knew? A little drink and she might wake one night to find him standing in her room…

'You could always leave the job,' Rafael continued thoughtfully. 'But, without any qualifications, how easy would it be for you to get a well-paid job to replace this? One that allowed you sufficient time to continue your studies? I've looked around here and the economy's good but there's heavy competition out there… lots of people with degrees pounding on office doors.' He paused, giving her time for his words to sink in. 'Your father would like to get to know you. If you had been in any way the sort of woman I thought would hurt him, I would not be standing here having this conversation with you. He…wants to get to know you and I, in turn, want to facilitate that.'

'Should I be flattered?' Sofia flung at him. 'It seems that lots of thought has gone into how *my father* would benefit from the arrangement, and how *you* would, but hey, what about me?'

'Oh, but I feel you should take time out to consider the advantages of accepting what's on offer, and the greatest of them is your freedom. Freedom from all of this. Think about it, Sofia. No having to do as you're told, with your free time whittled down to when it suits your employers. Take this deal and I will immediately begin transferring a healthy sum of money into your account. Whatever you want, you will be able to have. Shares in the company would go to me but, as compensation, you would receive a vast amount of money. No more scrimping and saving.'

'I could never marry you,' Sofia said weakly. She thought of her cousin, with all his problems, and her aunt who struggled daily to make ends meet. The little she handed over meant so much to them. How much more would she be able to do if money was no object? Expert physiotherapy for Miguel? An operation, perhaps? There were many cutting-edge treatments out there... More than that, she could move them to somewhere nicer, a house with a garden out in the suburbs where her aunt wouldn't feel scared if she happened to be walking home at night. There was so much she could do and the limitless possibilities hovered over her head, dazzling and seductive. 'You lied to me. You pretended to be someone you weren't. How could I ever marry someone I didn't even like?'

Rafael hesitated but only momentarily. 'This is a business deal. Marry me and in return you become a wealthy woman. As for the nature of our relationship...you will be free to do your own thing, as I will, within reason and with absolute discretion.' He lowered his eyes, shielding his expression, guarding his thoughts, doing what came naturally to a man as intensely private as he was.

For some reason, Rafael's cool, detached logic stung like heck. So he didn't fancy her and he never had. She'd been mistaken. Was she so full of herself that she'd actually thought that he'd been interested? Giving off all the right signals? Getting under her skin because he lusted after her the way she foolishly lusted after him?

'So what you're offering is…' Her voice was glacial.

'Yes.' Rafael met her eyes and held her gaze. 'The ultimate marriage of convenience.'

CHAPTER FOUR

WITH HIS BACK to the coffee shop, and a paper cup of over-stewed coffee in one hand, Rafael scanned the faces of the people emerging from Customs out into the waiting crowds. A few were optimistically peering to find loved ones. Most looked frazzled and weary.

Under normal circumstances, Rafael would not have been standing there, drinking mediocre coffee and waiting for anyone to arrive. Under normal circumstances, he would have dispatched his driver to do the honours, but these were hardly normal circumstances.

A fortnight ago, he had left Argentina an engaged man. He had presumed that Sofia would leave with him but, she'd informed him, she had things to do.

'I can't just up sticks and leave,' she had told him, sitting upright across from him in the formal sitting room where the details of this marriage of convenience had been discussed with the formality of two heads of state at a summit. 'I have things to do.'

'What things?'

'Things,' she had said coolly. 'All the usual things a person has to do just before they travel to another country to marry someone they barely know.'

'Thereby ensuring themselves a small fortune in the process,' Rafael had been prompted into saying, edgily. 'As a token of good faith, I'm prepared to personally transfer a sizeable amount to your bank account online right now, if you give me your account details.'

'I also,' Sofia had added, overriding the offer, 'don't like the idea of just disappearing and leaving a farewell note behind. I may not be the Walters' biggest fan,' she had conceded truthfully, 'but I'm fond of their children and I would like to say goodbye to them.'

So that had been that. In the end, it had worked out for the best because Rafael had travelled back solo and had taken the opportunity to explain the situation to David, who was now on the slow and laborious route to recuperation.

It had also given him ample opportunity to crystallise the *what happens next?* in the scenario.

Not that he hadn't thought about it while he had been out there. He had. Eventually. When matters had come to a head.

He'd been confronted with a sexy beauty and for a while his libido had misbehaved but, yes, when he had sat her down and explained the situation, he had known that acting on his libido was not going to do.

This wasn't going to be one of his transitory affairs. He wasn't going to be able to walk away after a handful of weeks and bouquet of 'it's over' flowers lovingly chosen by his PA.

No, Sofia Suarez, whose existence he hadn't been aware of a fortnight previously, was going to be slightly more long-lasting than that.

A year. That was the timeline mutually agreed as they had coolly and objectively discussed the nuts and bolts of their arrangement. A year, during which he would sort out the problem with Freddy and she would build the bonds with her father that would last beyond the inevitable divorce. A year seemed like a reasonable length of time. Having agreed to the deal, not once had she baulked, and he had admired her for that.

It was going to be a mutually beneficial situation for all concerned. For his godfather, who was desperate to meet his flesh-and-blood daughter. For him, because he was not only going to do something for the only human being on the planet he actually had time for but, in the process, would sort out the aggravation of his godfather's stepson's interference—and, as no miserly bonus, garner himself a healthy slice of the leisure industry his godfather had made his own. And of course for his bride-to-be, who would suddenly find herself one of the wealthiest women on the continent.

Joy and laughter all round.

But not if he allowed his libido to rule his head.

Rafael had felt the sizzle of attraction between them. He had seen the flare of desire in her feline green eyes and for a short while he had actually contemplated doing something about it. Because the pull towards her, forbidden fruit when he'd started thinking with his head instead of that other, far less reliable part of his body, was the strongest he'd ever experienced.

But this was a business arrangement and he had never been stupid enough to mix business with pleasure.

His solution had been the perfect one. They would maintain their freedom of movement whilst obeying rules of utmost discretion. A year was hardly an eternity in the great scheme of things.

Mind half-playing on the various formalities to be manoeuvred, Rafael spotted her emerging from the airport corridor through which lay Arrivals and Customs. She was walking slowly behind a family and trying hard to control a trolley that seemed determined to explore the opposite direction from the one she was taking.

Her long, dark, curly hair was tied back but travel had unravelled most of it from its restraints. She was dressed in a pair of faded jeans, a loose T-shirt and a scruffy bomber jacket. Her skin was the colour of latte and as smooth as silk and he drew in a sharp breath before briskly walking in her direction.

Just when you figure you've got life nicely under control, he thought with grim amusement, *you discover that life's decided to turn the tables and start controlling you.*

Just as well he was made of sterner stuff and could handle anything life decided to throw at him.

Flustered and bug-eyed, because she could count on the fingers of one hand the number of hours she had actually managed to sleep over the past couple of weeks, Sofia was not aware of Rafael's steady approach.

She was too busy trying not to crash into the three-year-old toddler being pulled along by his mother.

The dark timbre of Rafael's voice brought her to an abrupt stop, but not for long, because he seamlessly took the trolley from her and ushered her out of the steady stream of traffic looking for familiar faces.

'Good flight?' he enquired politely.

Sofia slanted a glance at him. Somehow she

had managed to forget just how stunning the guy was. So tall, so powerfully built, so aggressively masculine.

Eyes turned in his direction. Had he noticed? She was sure that he must have and that awareness of his own sexual magnetism would certainly account for some of his overwhelming self-assurance.

'Fine, thank you,' she returned, remembering for the record that he might be sex on legs but he was also someone who got what he wanted, whatever the cost and even if it involved lying.

'That's all the luggage you have with you?'

'I travel light.'

'Sensible. You're going to have a whole new wardrobe anyway, so the less of your old things you have to dispose of, the better.'

'How is my…my…how is David doing?'

'You're free to call him "Dad" if you like.'

'He's not my dad.'

Rafael shrugged but then turned to look down at her, his tone gentling. 'I understand the situation, Sofia. You're going to be meeting someone you have no interest in meeting but you're going to have to control the tendency to be waspish. David is recuperating but the last thing he needs is to be stressed out by surly behaviour.'

'You have no right to tell me off as though I'm a kid.' Sofia looked him squarely in the eyes. 'I didn't ask to be here.'

'But here you are, and I could name a million and one reasons why.' He looked at her wryly, eyebrows raised. 'Check your bank account and you'll get my drift.'

Face burning, Sofia looked away. He had sent her three emails. One contained a form, basically preventing her from blabbing to the press about *anything*. The other contained a complicated legal document involving distribution of shares and cash and she had signed it without reading it to the end.

The third email had detailed practical information. That one she had read thoroughly but now that she was here, so far from home, panic began to set in.

She rested her hand lightly on his arm as they emerged from the airport into cool spring air.

They had left some of the bustling crowds behind. Out here, cars were pulling up and slowly driving off, dropping and collecting passengers.

What have I got myself into? Sofia suddenly thought, terrified in a way she hadn't been back in the safety of her room at the Walters' mansion. Yes, she had agreed to something that made sound financial sense. He had assured her that theirs would not be a relationship in any true sense of the word and she had believed him. She was also, underneath the bluster, ever so slightly curious about the man who had fathered her, even though she doubted she could ever feel anything for some rich guy who had disappeared and broken her mother's heart.

But still…

Here she was, and her mouth was suddenly dry and her pulses racing all over the place.

'What is it?'

'I… I…' Her voice trailed off.

'The car is over there.' He nodded to a monstrously big Range Rover. 'You can get it off your chest once we're driving.'

'You sent an email,' Sofia began once she had climbed into the passenger seat and the car was silently exiting the cavernous car park. 'I'm afraid I've forgotten… I signed the stuff and I know…well…that we've given this a year, but was there anything else? And where…where are we going now? I feel I should have asked more questions but…'

'What did the boss say when you handed in your notice, just out of interest?'

'James?'

'I don't suppose he was happy about that.'

'It was inconvenient for both of them.' She flushed and looked away, recalling the angry gleam in James's eyes. She'd wondered whether he hadn't planned, at some point, to try to get her into bed, and was annoyed because the opportunity had removed itself from his grasp. He didn't intimidate her but she was seriously glad that he was no longer her boss.

'I'll bet. You're nervous and wondering whether you've done the right thing.'

'Have I said that?'

Rafael shot her a sideways look. 'Remember that talent of mine for reading what's not been said? If you're having doubts, then remember the boss whose nose was put out of joint when you handed in your notice. I saw that photo. I can recognise a sleaze ball from a mile away. Life would have become increasingly difficult for you there. The guy was probably circling like a shark. So, you asked where we're going. Right now, we're going to be staying at one of my houses outside London. Close enough for me to commute, at least on weekends, but far enough for you to find your feet far from prying eyes.'

'Prying eyes?'

'I've done my utmost to steer clear of paparazzi in both my professional and personal life and am only ever in print in connection with some of the more significant deals I've done over the years. On the whole, reporters have little to no interest in my personal life but, that said, the fact that I'm married isn't something that's going to pass unnoticed.' He paused and slanted another sideways glance at her. 'I thought you might want to adjust to life over here in relative peace and quiet before you're introduced as my wife. Hence we avoid my London base for a few weeks.'

'That's very thoughtful of you,' Sofia said stiffly.

'It will also enable you to control the occasions when you meet David. I've discussed this with him and he's happy with the arrangement. He is, believe it or not, as nervous about meeting you as you are of meeting him.'

'I'm not nervous.'

'I'll let that one pass. Have you ever been to this country before?'

'No.' She sighed and gazed out of the window at the soulless buzz of the motorway.

'You'll familiarise yourself with the place in time.' He paused. 'We're heading out of London at the moment. I've arranged a jeweller, who will be coming to my house with a selection of rings. You can take your pick of whatever you like. I've also had a timetable of various activities prepared for you, including a shopping trip for…amongst other things…a dress for the big day. You can either go to Harrods or else Harrods will come to you, if you don't fancy London.'

Sofia thought that this was the reality. The ring. The dress. A ceremony that suited all parties but had no emotional significance. The best that money could buy but without joy, anticipation or love.

She shivered and laughed unsteadily.

'What is it?' Rafael quizzed, not looking at her. 'I'm merely going over all the practical details.'

'I know. It's strange,' she said slowly, 'But for a while, when you first arrived at the Walters' house, when you were pretending to be a gardener, I actually felt comfortable with you. I hadn't expected to, but I did. You were...different. More easy going, light-hearted. I suppose that was just a persona and this is the real you.'

Rafael flushed darkly. 'I don't have a split personality, Sofia.'

'You weren't cold and distant like this...'

'I'm being practical,' he offered brusquely. 'It's the best way of dealing with this situation. This is not Argentina and it's better for the both of us if we approach it from the same perspective. We're in an arrangement and we need to view it as such.' He looked at her, at her smooth, stunningly sexy profile, the gentle curve of her neck, the sweep of her dark hair, and his body stirred in unwelcome and definitely inappropriate response. 'It's essential, in fact,' he felt compelled to stress in a roughened undertone.

Sofia didn't say anything but she was sitting next to a stranger.

'It's just a little weird to think that I'm about to embark on a wedding and a marriage to a guy who is more of a stranger now than he was when I first met him.'

'Not such a great idea to go there,' Rafael said, picking up pace now that the airport surroundings had been left behind and they were shooting away from the city. 'This is what we both signed up for and we both had our reasons. Let's just hit Acceptance Road and keep on it.'

'But don't you feel just a little bit sad that you're not getting married for all the *right* reasons?' She laughed lightly to cover up the sincerity of what she was saying. Funny thing was, she'd always considered herself the sort of practical girl who didn't have a romantic bone in her body. Not really. Yes, she believed in love, but a *sensible* sort of love. Not the sort of tempestuous carousel of emotion that had plagued her mother and driven her into relationships that had been doomed before they got off the ground.

'The right reasons being...the starry-eyed business of *true love*?' Rafael laughed shortly. 'In a word, no.' And just like that he thought of times past and his brief and disastrous foray into married life. Hell, he thought he'd relegated *that* slice of insanity to the past! Too young to know better and too green round the gills to re-alise that some women loved money more than they loved the men they claimed to adore. He shut the wayward memory down. You learned from the crap that was thrown at you and you moved on. He'd learned from having rich par-ents who hadn't given a damn about him and he'd moved on. He'd learned from that costly, juvenile mistake when he'd married in haste and he'd moved on.

'You're very cynical, aren't you?'

'Very realistic. I've seen where so-called *true love* ends up and it's not in a happy-ever-after scenario. I'm comfortable with this arrange-ment. And you should be too because, as we've agreed, there is a time limit to it.'

'I remember,' Sofia said dryly. One year, he

had concluded, during which time the relationship with David could be forged, the business of Freddy would be concluded and thereafter she would be free to divorce and pick back up her life, but as a wealthy woman.

'I didn't take you for the romantic kind,' he eventually remarked to break the silence and kill the remnants of uninvited memories. 'In fact, you were pretty spiky when we first met.'

'I'm not the romantic kind! And you were pretty arrogant when we first met, which was probably why I was spiky.' It was suddenly unnerving because he'd lost the cool voice, and that glimpse of the sexy, easy guy she'd found herself attracted to was back. It was just a glimpse but it was still enough to make her skin tingle. This time, though, she was prepared and she quickly changed the subject because there was no way she was going to lose her head a second time round. He'd turned the charm on when he'd descended in his fake role as gardener because he'd needed to suss her out, get to know her, and that had been the most efficient way of doing itt. But charm was inherent in his personality and she guessed that it would be far too easy to fall victim to it again. It was something she wasn't about to do.

'When...er...do I get to meet...er...?'

'David?' Rafael half-smiled. 'Scheduled for the day after tomorrow. Saturday. He'll be back in his house and up to visitors, although any visit will have to be brief. And the big day... the following Saturday. It'll be a suitably small affair. Thereafter, we'll be man and wife— although, as I've said, I'll be working in London during the week and on weekends you might want to travel down and stay in my apartment...handy for setting up a routine of visits to David once he's home.'

No time together was what Sofia read into that statement of fact, and it came as no great shock, as he'd previously sketched out that scenario.

'So I'll be out in the sticks during the week.' She would carry on with her studies. She'd enjoy the discipline, even though she wouldn't need the job at the end of it. She would explore her surroundings, maybe do something crafty with her spare time, volunteer somewhere or maybe just see what sports were on offer. It would be a life she had never envisioned but she would need something to do for herself while she was here.

'Unless you prefer my apartment. It's more than big enough for the both of us.'

'Won't that be an intrusion?' Sofia murmured inaudibly, because she'd already worked out that if Rafael spent the week away from her it would give him ample opportunity to continue uninterrupted in whatever life he had involving the opposite sex.

She thought of him with another woman and was shocked at the raw sting of jealousy that swept through her in a tidal wave.

'Come again?'

'Nothing,' she said brightly. 'Just…enjoying the scenery and…being somewhere different.'

The car ate up the miles and, despite the flurry of nervous tension inside her, she really did enjoy the scenery as the roads became less congested and the land more open, rolling in a patchwork quilt of different colours on either side of the dual carriageway until they cut away from the main drag.

Then they drove up smaller roads, narrower

streets that opened into tiny villages announcing themselves with a single signpost. She saw lots of greenery and lots of trees and then, eventually, the car swerved slowly through electronically controlled wrought-iron gates.

This wasn't what she'd been expecting. The drive opened out to a small courtyard and then an elongated cottage that was picture-perfect. White walls, clambering ivy, roses.

'You *own* this house?'

Rafael drew to a stop and flashed her a smile of such utter charm that for a few seconds she struggled to breathe.

The worst of it was that he didn't even realise the effect that smile could have on her.

'Investment,' he said succinctly. 'Apparently out here old and quaint sells. As it happens, I've hung onto it far longer than I originally planned, because David's always enjoyed coming out here, but in the meantime it's done very nicely indeed pricewise. That answer your question?'

'Perfectly.'

There was a snazzy black car in the drive and

now an attractive blonde in her mid-thirties emerged and walked towards the Range Rover.

'The ring selection,' Rafael murmured, reaching across her to snap open the door and pausing before withdrawing his arm that was inches from her breasts. 'For the love-struck couple, giddy after their whirlwind romance.'

'Is that what everyone thinks?'

Rafael shrugged. 'David knows the ins and outs, and Freddy has already begun to make outraged noises, but I'd say the rest of the world probably think that this is the real deal. Why wouldn't they? I honestly don't care but it might be easier all round for you to give as few people as little to talk about.'

Sofia was trying hard to concentrate on every word he was saying but her eyes were compulsively looking at his well-defined, sensual mouth and her body was way too aware of that arm of his almost but not quite brushing her breasts.

She barely saw the rings, which were a blur of diamonds and gold, small, glittering objects that mocked all the principles she had ever stood by. They nestled against the black velvet and all she could think was *this should be for real*. In front of them, the attractive blonde was positively throbbing with excitement.

Sofia pointed to the smallest and least ostentatious and felt the light touch of Rafael's hand cupping the nape of her neck, gently massaging beneath her mane of hair. Time felt suspended. She inhaled and then found it almost impossible to exhale because every nerve in her body, every pulse, was caught in a whirlpool of dark, swirling sensation.

'Way too small, my darling,' he murmured, leaning forward, his hand still massaging her neck, to point at a far bigger diamond. Then he drew back and his hand dropped, but only to lightly rest on her waist.

'Lucky you,' the blonde whispered when the ordeal was at an end and rings had been selected, ready for adjustments before the big day.

'Oh, yes.' Sofia glanced to where Rafael was now standing to one side, on his phone talking work, safely out of range of her rebellious body. 'I'm the luckiest girl in the world.'

As she said that, he looked at her, dark eyes

tangling with bright green, and hot colour crawled into her cheeks.

Did she look like a genuine blushing bride-to-be? She hoped not and, to dispel any such illusion, she stood up briskly, smile pinned to her face, and ushered the woman out. Then she asked whether she could explore her surroundings.

'Take your time,' Rafael drawled. 'I have some work to do. I'll be in the kitchen.'

He vanished through one of the opened doors towards the back and Sofia knew that this was how it was going to be until such time as the marriage drew to its inevitable conclusion, leaving her a rich woman free to go her own way.

She did as told and explored. She took her time and, in the process, she fell in love with the sprawling, well-decorated house. She never imagined that she would actually live in a place like this. The proportions of the rooms were perfect, the muted tones exquisite, the furnishings luxurious. Whatever she'd traded, whatever dreams she'd locked away, she knew that the deal done had given her all sorts of advantages she could never, ever have achieved on her own.

She didn't even have to pretend to be head-over-heels in love with Rafael. Mutual respect was what was on the table.

And what, exactly, had she left behind? Her infrastructure in Argentina had been almost non-existent thanks to all the travelling she'd done with her mother over the years. She'd lost touch with school friends. She only had her aunt and her cousin. Her heart constricted when she thought about them because she would miss them but, as she'd told Misa, it wasn't going to be for ever and she would be able to do so much for Miguel.

'Love isn't the be all and end all,' she had said with genuine honesty. 'Mum had her heart broken because of love and then spent the rest of her life trying to relocate it and failing. Life would have been a lot easier if she'd just focused on…other things. Financial security. A steady job.'

She had already set up a standing order and had told her aunt to start looking around for a better property, suitably adapted for Miguel.

She'd explained the situation, the practicalities of it. She had fought down the lump in her throat that somehow her aunt would be disappointed she had told herself that this was what mattered. Not big dreams of fairy-tale romances but the solid advantages of financial security.

She still believed all of that and it was frustrating to find herself doubting those long-held convictions.

On the spur of the moment, she dialled her aunt's number, gently pushing the door to the upstairs bedroom behind her.

The minute Rafael had come clean about his intentions, she had slammed down the shutters and any temptation to confide further details of her private life had screeched to a halt.

She'd always been so protective of her privacy and she had been appalled that she'd begun opening up to a complete stranger who had turned out to be a fraud.

Her aunt answered on the first ring and, just like that, Sofia was transported back to Buenos Aires and the gruelling, repetitive life Misa led, doing her utmost to make everything more comfortable for Miguel.

It was a life that was so different from the one she now found herself transported to that it was scarcely believable.

In a low voice, smiling when she thought of all the possibilities that would open up to the only relative she knew and someone she loved, Sofia described the very house in which she was standing, describing the trip over and the car that had collected her. She peered through the window, down to a rambling garden that matched the house.

Trees fringed the back and beyond those trees were rolling fields. Borders of flowers and shrubs were artfully entwined and under a drooping willow was a wooden bench, perfect for reading.

Still smiling, she turned to find Rafael standing in the doorway, his expression unreadable, his dark eyes cool and speculative.

She ended the call, flushing and annoyed with herself, because she had nothing to feel guilty about and yet she did.

'Personal call?' he asked, strolling into the

room and joining her by the window through which he peered absently before turning around to look at her. 'Call you felt you had to make with the door shut?'

Sofia opened her mouth to tell him that she had been touching base with her aunt but stopped herself.

She'd decided to share as little as possible, hadn't she? She had no intention of telling him how she planned to use some of the money that had landed into her account. He had made it clear that this was purely a business transaction, that he would lead his life as he saw fit just so long as he kept the details of what he was up to to himself.

Confidences were the business of friends. He wasn't her friend, despite what she might originally have thought.

Besides, what if he decided to have a say in where her money went? Could he do that? Did he care one way or the other? It was best not to risk anything.

She couldn't trust him and it was just as well to remember that.

She shrugged, slipping the mobile phone into her over the shoulder bag.

'If you have any ties you think I should know about,' Rafael drawled, with just the tiniest edge in his voice, 'then you should think about telling me now.'

'Ties?'

'I asked you once whether you were involved with anyone out there and you told me that you weren't.'

'Oh, I see what you mean, Rafael. Men.' She lowered her eyes, torn between telling him the truth and protecting a life she felt he had no right to know about, just as there would be huge tracts of his life he felt she had no right to know about, whatever their marital status.

'No men. At least…' She thought of Miguel and hardened her jaw. 'You don't have to worry on that front, although if I recall you did say that we could lead separate lives…err…when it came to that kind of thing.'

She began moving away and he caught her by her arm, halting her.

'That's what you intend on doing?' he asked softly, stepping fractionally closer to her.

Her heart was beating fast. Her pulses were racing and her whole nervous system was in free fall.

A passing touch and she was going to pieces! She couldn't tear her eyes away from his mouth and the feel of his hand on her arm was electric.

'I… I don't know what I intend on doing,' Sofia said breathlessly, inching away as much as she could.

'I won't tolerate any affair being flaunted in my face,' he said flatly.

'Nor will I!' Her green eyes flashed and suddenly there was an outpouring of emotion only weakly held in check by the stern lectures she had given herself ever since she had embarked on this road. 'Whatever you might think of me, this was never what I envisaged for myself when it came to marriage! Yes, I know all about those *million and one reasons* for going through with it, and yes, I know it's not going to last for ever and I'll walk away with lots of money in my bank account. But it still hurts to know that I'm going to tie the knot with some guy who will play around with other women and do his own thing!'

She looked at him fiercely. She felt herself gathering momentum. 'Furthermore, this is *your* territory. You're established here and you don't care what the world thinks of you or the choices you make! But I... I don't belong here, so just try and imagine what it'll feel like if I ever walk into a room to be confronted by some woman you're bedding behind my back!'

'You have quite the imagination...'

'Have I? You might not intend on flaunting anything but are you going to tell me that that world you occupy isn't a really small one?'

'It's small,' Rafael admitted in a roughened undertone. His grasp on her arm had slackened but he had also closed the tiny distance between them so that she could feel the heat radiating from his body.

'Women can be vicious,' Sofia muttered, looking down and thinking of the nasty digs that had plagued her teenage years and the bitchiness of jealous girls who had always guarded their stupid boyfriends against what they'd seen as a possible threat. As if she'd ever been interested in any of them. But still she knew what it felt like to be attacked through no fault of her own.

She shuddered at the thought of having to deal with some woman Rafael might be seeing.

'Are you speaking from experience?' he murmured, dropping his hand to his side and stepping back as he stared down at her with his head tilted to one side.

'The fairer sex can be anything but gentle when it comes to certain things.' Sofia tilted her head at a challenging angle and folded her arms. Her whole body was still tingling. She felt as though she'd been touched, intimately touched, even though all he'd done was circle her arm with his fingers.

'Especially given the way you look,' he said, eyes roving over her flushed face. 'I get it, *cara.*'

Thick silence greeted this observation. It stretched and stretched, sending her thoughts into a giddy tailspin, making her mouth dry. It was an effort not to close her eyes and reach up…just a little…enough to brush her lips against his mouth.

Her nipples, pushing against the cotton bra,

felt scratchy and over-sensitive and between her legs…felt hot and damp.

Their eyes locked. His breathing was thick and fast, giving her signals she didn't trust and didn't want to understand. He took a step towards her, jaw clenched, his body rigid with tension.

Then, just like that, he seemed to gather himself, shutting down an atmosphere that had flared up between them like a sudden, fierce conflagration.

'Right now…' His voice was jerky and he raked his fingers through his hair, looking briefly away but then directing his back to her flushed face. 'We both have enough on our plate without imagining a situation that might or might not happen.'

He walked towards the window, stared out with his back to her and then threw over his shoulder, 'Now that you've seen where you'll be living, I think we can head back to London. The house should have been ready for you to move in immediately, and I would have returned to London, but there's been a mix-up with the housekeeper who needs to come in tomorrow to spruce the place up. It would be useful for you to spend the day tomorrow buying whatever clothes you think you might need, anyway. I'll also make sure you have a car at your disposal. You name the make and the model. When it comes to what happens… outside this marriage…that is a bridge to be crossed in due course, so let's stick to the present. Meet the parents—or should I say *parent*—wedding vows exchanged, and once that's done I get going on sorting out the problem with Freddy. That's enough to be going on with, wouldn't you agree?'

CHAPTER FIVE

WHERE THE HELL was she?

Rafael looked at his watch again. So far, she was half an hour late and counting, and he was beginning to think that he should have taken control of this final big step. Should have insisted that he bring her here to the Register Office himself. At the very least, get his driver to collect her from the house in the country where she had been spending the past week, bar that one day when she had shopped in London at his suggestion.

But then what was the chance that she would have allowed herself to be chivvied into doing what he wanted?

Rafael grimaced, mentally acknowledging that when he had set off on his mission to make her acquaintance the last thing he'd expected was to discover someone with a will as stubborn as his own.

She had turned down all offers from him to get someone—his PA or one of his other, trusted employees—to show her around London.

'I learned how to be independent a long time ago,' she had said flatly. 'I can manage just fine on my own.'

She had openly scoffed at his concerns that she might find herself in an unsafe situation because she had no idea where the no-go areas were.

Her one worry—and he knew this from the shadow that flitted across her face when he mentioned it—was meeting her father, but she had been spared that because David had not been able to see her after all. A series of gruelling tests had left him depressed and, once again, hospital-bound. He had been discharged the day before but he was still in a wheelchair.

Rafael glanced down at his godfather, patiently waiting for his daughter to appear bounding up the steps of the impressive Town Hall.

David Dunmore looked his age. He was no longer the sharp-eyed, rotund father figure of old. He had lost a substantial amount of weight, something Rafael was noticing for the first time, and his face was weary and drawn. He looked *fragile*. For a man who had once been so vital, so energised, so *big*, this fragility was a sucker punch to the gut.

Rafael cursed softly under his breath because the last thing his godfather needed was for Sofia to decide that she couldn't go through with the deal after all.

And how did he know that that wasn't exactly what had happened?

She already had a huge amount of cash in her bank account. Nothing like the amount she could expect to land eventually, but enough to hightail it back to Argentina and set up camp to a very high standard indeed.

He had trusted her to sign on the dotted line and follow through, because his gut instinct told him that she was trustworthy, but there was always a first when it came to gut instincts going wrong.

On the verge of whipping out his mobile phone and calling her, a hurrying figure caught the corner of his eye and he half-turned in its direction.

And there she was.

The breath left him in a rush, as if he'd been punched in the gut.

In the warmth of a mild-mannered spring day, with crowds scurrying all around, she was a vision of such unparalleled beauty that he was forcibly and unpleasantly reminded of just how tempting a creature she was. From the first time he'd laid eyes on her his libido had started misbehaving, and it was misbehaving now, even though he had already told himself that the best course of action was the very one he had taken: to keep things purely on a business level, thereby avoiding unnecessary complications. He'd stated his case and made sure that she was on the same page…

But, hell…when a woman looked the way she did…

She had forgone white or cream, or any variation thereof, and was wearing a figure-hugging lilac dress that somehow managed to be extremely proper and outrageously sexy at the same time.

He had only seen her informally dressed and she hid her assets well.

Not so now. Her generous breasts made a mockery of the high, prissy neckline, just as her shapely legs made a mockery of the knee length cut of the dress. The single string of pearls around her neck sent his mind screaming off in all sorts of inappropriate directions.

He wondered what they would look like against her naked, latte-coloured body.

Her long, streaming hair was neatly tied back and his fingers itched to unravel it from its restraints.

Irritated with himself for a physical weakness he didn't seem able to control at all, Rafael placed both hands on his godfather's shoulders and leant down to draw his attention to the hurrying figure.

For the moment, it was simply the three of them, with his loyal, middle-aged PA there to sign as one of the witnesses, but after the brief ceremony they would be joined by a small selection of friends, and of course Freddy, where a late lunch would be had in the private room of one of the most expensive Michelin-starred restaurants in the City.

Expression veiled, Rafael watched the bounce of her breasts and wanted nothing more than to scrap the expensive lunch, take her to a hotel room and bed her.

It was a crazy, wayward desire that he clamped down with iron determination.

'You're here,' was all he said when she was finally standing in front of him. 'I was beginning to wonder whether you'd make it at all. Sofia…meet your father…'

Sofia's heart was beating so fast she felt she might pass out at any moment.

She was nearly forty minutes late. There had been no need for her to be late at all because she had left herself plenty of time to make the trip to the Register Office, even though she hadn't done herself any favours by turning down the offer of Rafael's driver.

Pride.

But somehow everything had been just a little bit delayed, from having to hunt down the pearl necklace, which hadn't been where she had thought it was, to stupid little glitches with transport.

But here she was.

She felt sick.

The old man looking up at her from a wheel-chair was far more frail than she had expected. Was she supposed to launch into excited bab-ble? Start a long-winded conversation? Put on a show of filial excitement?

Sofia felt like doing none of those things be-cause this was the guy who had dumped her mother, sending her into a downward spiral from which she never really recovered.

'Hello,' she said neutrally, stepping back and pointedly not offering an outstretched hand.

'My dear, dear girl. You're even more beau-tiful than I could have expected. I cannot tell you what a joy it is to have you here.'

Sofia glanced down, intensely uncomfortable, and even more so when she noted the glimmer of tears in his eyes.

She immediately looked up at Rafael, then wished she hadn't, because she just couldn't seem to see him without her heart doing all sorts of stupid things.

This was not a traditional wedding and they had both interpreted that glaring fact in their own way. She by wearing a simple lilac dress that could multi-task, so it wouldn't end up hanging in her wardrobe never to be worn again, and he by wearing a pair of linen trousers and a white shirt which was loosely cuffed to the elbows. He looked so spectacular that her mouth instantly went dry and she felt in desperate need of a glass of water.

'Apologies if I've kept you all waiting.' She turned to his PA, whom she'd briefly met on her one and only day spent shopping in London, and made some idle chat, but not for long because they were on a timetable that was threatening to be scuppered by her late arrival.

No time, thankfully, to address that emotional greeting from David, even though she could sense him looking at her as they entered the building. She wanted to look back at him, see if she could spot any resemblances to her, but at the same time she didn't want to show interest. A lifetime of writing him out of her life was tailoring her responses.

No time to get lost in Rafael, which only

ended up leading to the sort of edge-of-seat nervous tension that infuriated her because she knew just the sort of guy he was.

Just enough time to be dimly aware of the words that united them, then he was slipping the ring on her finger.

She stared down and her heart thumped and her head emptied of all thought. He tilted her chin so that she was gazing up at him and for a few seconds the whole world shrank to just the two of them. Then his lips grazed hers and she thought, *this is just for show, for the PA who doesn't know the situation...* But those lips were awakening all kinds of responses in her. He darted his tongue into her parted mouth and her breathing quickened. She wanted to clutch the material of his shirt. Instead, she pulled back. He released her immediately and the moment was gone as she turned and the watching faces came back into focus as she walked towards them.

She felt the dry, light touch of David's hand covering hers and she stole a tight-lipped look at him, hearing him murmur how pleased he was to finally meet her.

Sofia quietly removed her hand and offered a stiff smile, not quite knowing what to say.

'And I'm sure,' Rafael murmured smoothly, ushering her out of the room by the elbow, 'that the feeling is returned. Isn't it, Sofia?'

'Of course,' she said dutifully, not bothering to conceal her insincerity, and ignoring Rafael's frown of disapproval. She was here but that didn't mean that she was obliged to wipe the past out and pretend that everything was hunky dory.

Outside, two Range Rovers were waiting to ferry them to the restaurant. She stood politely while her father was helped into the first one, with Rafael's PA, and then she and her newly acquired husband were in the back of the other, and Rafael immediately turned to her and said, *sotto voce*, 'Not going to do.' How was it that for a fleeting moment in time he'd actually forgotten what this sham was all about?

'What isn't?' Her eyes drifted to his mouth and then, embarrassed, she looked down to the taut pull of trousers over his muscular thighs.

'You know what I'm talking about, Sofia. David wants to forge a connection with you.'

'What if I don't want to forge a connection with him?'

'Then you're going to have to make a sterling effort to pretend.'

'What's the point of doing that, Rafael? I know I'm being well paid for the job, but pretending to feel something for someone I don't know from Adam isn't part of the brief.'

'Oh, but it is, *cara*.'

Sofia shivered because this was delivered with just a hint of silky threat.

'What do you mean?' she quizzed tartly.

'Here's what I mean. You're not going to avoid seeing David or treat him with disrespect. In any way, shape or form.'

'I wasn't doing that.'

'He's asking you questions. You're going to answer them, and you're going to do a damn good job of answering them with a smile on your face as opposed to the grimace of someone swallowing shards of glass.'

'But I...' She dragged her eyes away and stared straight ahead to the other Range Rover in front of them. 'You don't understand.'

'What don't I understand?'

'My mum and I were a team. I can't say that I enjoyed moving around, and I can't say that I had a lot of time for her falling in and out of love with good-looking guys who used her and then walked away, but we managed—and we managed without David Dunmore on the scene because he's never *been* on the scene. You can't just fabricate interest in someone because you happen to find out that you're related to them. That's not how it works.'

'Maybe not,' Rafael unbent sufficiently to say quietly. 'But look on this as a humane gesture. My godfather, your father, has been through the mill with his health. A further barrage of tests this week has reduced him to a person I scarcely recognise. He's holding on to the prospect of getting to know you like a drowning man clinging to a lifebelt. It's in your power to alleviate some of his depression by, at least, being civil. Can you honestly tell me that you're so selfish that you won't do that?'

Sofia flushed darkly and wondered what he would say if he knew that the depressed elderly man had once been an arrogant forty-something who had not hesitated to dump her mother, having strung her along, eventually making her pregnant. Not, in all fairness, that he had known about the pregnancy, although if he *had* known would the situation have been any different?

'Why do you care so much?' she asked, curiosity forcing a way past her resentment.

Rafael flushed. 'He's my godfather. Of course I care.'

'There's no *of course* about it,' Sofia returned drily. 'And somehow I can't see you as the sort of person who shows affection for someone because other people expect it.' But she could sense that when it came to David all was not as clear cut as for other people. When it came to his godfather, Rafael was vulnerable, and that realisation softened something inside her, endearing him to her in ways she couldn't define.

Rafael relaxed, his lean, intensely aggressive features softening into something approaching a smile.

'What are you trying to say?' Dark eyes glanced over to her as he sat sprawled against the door, his long legs eating up the space between them in the back of the car, as though too big to be comfortable in any restraining space.

'That you don't care what anyone thinks. You've told me so yourself.' She hesitated. It would be easy if she could see him as a one-dimensional cardboard cut-out, but she couldn't, and the second she tried to she was ambushed by all sorts of conflicting feelings because he was simply so complex. 'So why are you so… close to David? How is it that he's your god-father?'

'You ask a lot of questions.'

'I'm your wife,' Sofia was quick to respond. 'And, if you can tell me what to do and how I should behave, then the least I should be able to do, by way of returning the favour, is to try and find out a bit about *my husband*.' She looked at him with arched eyebrows and he grinned, then laughed appreciatively.

'Whatever our marriage is,' he drawled, 'boring it won't be.'

'Because I have a mind of my own and I'm not afraid to speak it?' She sniffed, disarmed by that smile.

'Amongst other things.'

'Well?'

She twisted the rose-gold ring on her finger. It felt so odd.

She was married to this big, powerful guy…a guy who commanded attention wherever he went. Eyes followed him whenever he entered a room—people wondered whether they should recognise him because he stood out… Even as a lowly gardener he had commanded her attention. *Here, in his stamping ground, he was the king of the jungle.*

'Well, if you insist on the back story, David was my grandfather's closest friend. They went to university together. Neither had much to speak of but David was the first to secure a bank loan and he used some of it to lend a hand to my grandfather, who then went on to do great things in import and export. David opened up a small hotel on the outskirts of the university town they both went to. Fill a gap, was David's reasoning. Something small but classy for relatives visiting kids at the university. He'd studied economics and figured that that was the most lucrative way to put his degree to good use.

'Roll on ten years and that one small hotel had expanded into a healthy dozen or so, at which point he began diversifying, going into different areas...exploring boutique hotels in far-flung places not yet on the tourist radar, dabbling in computer technology before computer technology had taken off. All from one small idea.'

Rafael shook his head and Sofia detected admiration in his dark eyes. 'He's always been the finest example of how to work your way to the top on your own merit. You could say that this is the stuff that mentors are made of.' He shot her a crooked smile but she saw past that. Rafael wasn't being ironic. He was being utterly truthful. In all aspects, David was larger than life to him, had been there for him in more ways than one.

That, she thought, lay at the heart of Rafael's devotion. Love, admiration, respect. Three powerful emotions. Cold as he was when it came to the business of love and marriage, he wasn't an ice-man, though she wasn't sure he would have agreed with her. He was far too fond of thinking of himself as infallible. He didn't see that great love, even if it wasn't of the romantic kind, made him as human as the next man.

Sofia frowned. 'He was in Argentina...'

'Taking over two hotels, turning them into something more visionary.'

Sofia thought that he must have been an extremely charismatic and dynamic guy, hence why her mother had fallen head over heels in love.

'So...your father was close to him as well?'

'My parents would have chosen David because they were probably in a hurry and needed someone to step into the role, if only to please my traditional grandparents. I suspect David worked as a godfather figure because he was based in the UK and available for babysitting duties while they busied themselves exploring anything and everything the universe had to offer. They were young, they were rich and they weren't going to let a kid hold them back.'

Detecting a thread of bitterness beneath that flatly spoken statement, Sofia looked at him, her curiosity at fever pitch now. She felt as though, through a miniscule crack, she was seeing a sliver of this man that hinted at depths hitherto keep hidden, and that glimpse was sufficient to awaken a thirst to find out more.

She shouldn't care, because they meant nothing to one another, but she found that she did.

The realisation filled her with a certain amount of unease, because curiosity was definitely not part of the package, but she couldn't help herself.

'So they travelled a lot,' she murmured, in a voice that melded encouragement with mild interest. She smiled. 'A bit like me, but I suppose the circumstances were slightly different. I expect they were probably travelling in style. Horse and carriage, where we were side-of-road and thumbs out.'

The grin returned. 'You make me laugh, you know that? You're also the master of understatement, Sofia.'

The lazy teasing in his voice brought colour to her cheeks and she smiled back at him. 'Travelling in style would be a lot less arduous than taking pot luck wherever you happened to land.'

'Oh, my parents travelled in style, all right.'

'Did you enjoy the experience as much as I did?' The sarcasm in her voice made him laugh.

'I wasn't dragged along in their wake, thankfully. They were about as responsible as a pair of kids without a care in the world, but they had the common sense to put me in a boarding school as soon as they feasibly could, and before that I was looked after, largely, by my grandparents.'

'How old were you when you were sent to boarding school?' she queried, unable to conceal her surprise.

'Seven.' Rafael's dark eyes collided with her wide, green ones and he laughed with genuine amusement. 'Are you about to tell me that you feel sorry for me? Don't waste your breath. I was very happy there. I spent holidays with my grandparents and then, later on, with David after my grandparents emigrated to South Africa.'

'And your parents?'

Rafael's mouth thinned.

Was he even aware of the signals he gave off? Sofia wondered. Was he even aware of the message he was sending underneath the casual, indifferent front? She didn't want to be sucked into his personality, the way she had been before she'd known who he really was, but she could feel her heart twisting when she thought about his circumstances as a child. In their different ways, they had both had to fight against the challenges they had been born into.

'My parents were killed when I was thirteen. Light-aeroplane crash. My father had bought it and they were having fun up in the clouds when it went into a tailspin from which it couldn't recover.'

'I… I don't know what to say. That's awful. I'm so very sorry for you, Rafael.'

'We're here.'

Sofia glanced away from his stern, brooding face to see that they were, indeed, outside the sort of exclusive restaurant that barely had to announce itself because anybody who was anybody should know where it was.

The conversation had ended and she had no idea how to retrieve it, even though she wanted to.

He held her hand walking in, absently stroking her thumb with his finger, but she knew that that was just for effect because only David knew the truth. Everyone else had bought into the fairy-tale whirlwind romance. She knew that but there was still a second when it felt *real*, a real *relationship* with real hopes and dreams. She didn't look at him but tentatively stroked his finger back and wondered whether she'd imagined it when he seemed to still for a fraction of a second.

Ahead of them, David had been positioned in his wheelchair at the long table and she saw, with a sinking heart, that there was an empty chair next to his, which she assumed was meant for her, with Rafael on the other side of her.

She barely had time to take in the rest of the people there. There was a handful. A couple of dozen at most. A no-fuss wedding which would have made complete sense to everyone there, given Rafael's intensely private personality. A splashy affair, weirdly, would have had everyone peering through the net curtains and wondering what was going on.

Introductions were made. The room was entirely private so there were no prying eyes and

Sofia knew that she was being assessed neutrally by everyone there: Rafael's PA, three company directors, friends of David, several attractive, younger couples, friends of Rafael, and the pesky stepson, whose destiny was about to change thanks to this marriage of convenience.

Freddy's blue eyes were narrowed and hostile but he didn't say a word as she walked past him towards the chair that was waiting for her. So he had his doubts…? Would Rafael's arm round her waist still those doubts? Did she look like a woman in love? Certainly, as Rafael's hand sent heat pouring through her, she knew that she resembled a blushing bride, even if the blushing was for the wrong reasons!

It was almost a relief to sit, even though it was next to her father, and, with the conversation gradually resuming as waiters entered and began doing their thing, she reluctantly began paying attention to the guy with whom her mother had fallen crazily in love.

'Just ignore the lot of them,' he whispered, leaning towards her, and she was forced to lean towards him just to pick up what he was saying. 'And, if you're nervous, then the champagne is exquisite. Best money can buy. Well known for its calming qualities. I would be sampling some myself, but unfortunately my consultant has been gloomy in his warnings.'

Sofia sipped some champagne and sneaked a glance at her father, who was formally dressed in a suit and tie. He looked gaunt but his eyes were sharp. She could see the powerhouse behind the diminished exterior.

'I don't want to be here,' she muttered, well aware that Rafael couldn't hear a word she was saying, because he was distracted by the woman next to him. Instead of recoiling, David leant even closer towards her.

'I know, my dear. It saddens me to think that the only reason you're occupying that seat is because you have been generously paid to do so.'

Sofia flushed, knowing how that made her sound.

'I'm no gold-digger,' she interjected, leaning into him to make herself heard.

'No one ever said you were, my dear. Money is always handy and, believe me, I don't blame you in the slightest for taking what was on offer.

You'd rather not have anything to do with me,
I realise that, but I hope very much that you'll
give it a go.'

She had his nose. Straight and small. And she
had the same shape of face—oval, where her
mother's had been girlishly elfin. Even without analysing it too much, she could see the
strength of her father's features in herself and
it was disconcerting.

'I'm only here because I didn't have a choice,'
she said in a low, defensive tone, hating the
fact that this man might think that she was just
another money-grabbing stranger happy to do
something she resented because she wanted
money in her bank account. That she was willing to sell her pride for the sake of hard cash.

'My godson can be very persuasive.'

'Your godson is a pain in the ass.' She pictured that dark, sinfully seductive face and
scowled. Next to her, David wheezed with sudden mirth and then promptly drank some water
to subdue the resulting coughing fit.

'Tell that to his face, and he might die of
shock because no one will ever have said that
to him before.'

'That's a shame,' Sofia retorted tartly, finally paying attention to the delicate titbits on her plate, a selection of mouth-watering tiny pastries with exotic fillings. 'If someone *had*, then maybe he wouldn't be so…so…arrogant and *infuriating.*' She flashed a sideways glance at her father who looked right back at her, speculatively.

'So you're not here because of Rafael's powers of persuasion…'

'My aunt needs financial assistance,' Sofia confessed. They were in a huddle. Heaven only knew, they must look like long-lost friends to outside eyes. 'My cousin, Miguel, was injured in an accident when he was sixteen and she's never had the money to properly care for him. That's why I'm here. That's the *only* reason I'm here.' She dug into the food. Yes, she had been harsh in stating the truth, but life was harsh.

'I didn't know,' David murmured mildly.

'Why would you? Oh, yes, I remember. You had me checked out.'

She slanted a sideways glare at him, ready to go into battle with this guy she had no time for, even if it meant rousing Rafael's displeasure, but David was once again smiling.

'Best thing I ever did.' He chortled. 'You're a tonic, my dear girl, a tonic.' He turned to face the assembled crowd and banged his fork sharply on the table until everyone fell silent.

'To the married couple,' he toasted, raising his glass. 'I dare say a sip of champagne for the toast won't kill me! And I thankfully don't have my consultant here to argue the point.' Laughter greeted this and Sofia couldn't help smiling. He looked at her slyly and winked. 'Let's raise our glasses to my very dear Rafael and his beautiful wife and my daughter, Sofia, away for too long but here now to stay. Long may they be happily united!'

Sofia tried not to choke on her champagne and when she caught Rafael's eye it was to see that he was trying hard not to burst out laughing.

CHAPTER SIX

THE LUNCH LASTED three hours, at the end of which Sofia had drunk far too much champagne. Nervous tension had not mixed well with the alcohol, and as she waited kerbside with Rafael for his driver to show up the thought of taking a train back to the cottage was almost unthinkable. She felt sick.

'Congratulations.' Rafael, having dispatched the last of the guests, turned to her with a wry expression.

'For what?'

'You made my godfather laugh. Don't know what you were saying, but whatever it was it was doing the trick.'

He channelled her into the back seat of the Range Rover and then angled his body so that he was looking right at her, his long legs loosely sprawled, his hands resting lightly on his thighs.

'I wasn't cracking any jokes.'

Restless and excruciatingly aware of him sitting so close to her, she anxiously twisted the rings round and round her finger, choosing to stare through the window of the car rather than look at him, but she was all too conscious of this drop-dead gorgeous guy next to her, all too alert of the way her body had reacted when he had touched it.

She was married and, even if it was a marriage in name alone, her blood still thickened with inexplicable heat at the thought.

Marriage was the one thing her mother had craved and never managed to attain. All things considered, she didn't think her mother would have been whooping with joy on behalf of her daughter. A marriage of convenience would not have sat well with a woman who'd believed in romance and fairy tales, even if none of them had managed to come true for her.

She slid her eyes across at him and her pulses quickened. Her brain wanted to box this up and neatly label it as the business deal it was, but her body wasn't falling into line. Her body was too aware of the ring on her finger and all the grey areas that highlighted.

Looking down, she was startled when she felt the light brush of Rafael's finger under her chin.

'Look at me,' he encouraged softly.

'What?' She jerked back but their eyes locked, and she found she couldn't tear her gaze away.

She'd ended up paying little attention to him during the meal. She'd been conscious of him, but her father had consumed her attention. Now, Rafael, *her husband*, seemed to suck the oxygen out of the atmosphere, leaving her breathless and acutely aware of his intense, smouldering masculinity.

The other guests—stepbrother, with whom she had barely exchanged a glance, aside—had been young and attractive. Several of the women had been attached to typical corporate-looking types and had been effusive and welcoming, eager to please the man who made sure their husbands were handsomely paid. Others, like the striking, dark-skinned woman who'd sat next to Rafael, with whom he had been discussing business for most of the meal, had clearly been colleagues.

'You did well. If you were nervous, then you did a good job of hiding it.'

'Isn't that part and parcel of the game we're playing?' She looked at him, hating herself, because she knew that there had been instances when it had felt way too real for comfort.

And she knew why. Scratch the surface and you'd find a woman still yearning to touch her forbidden husband.

She sighed and gave him a clear-eyed gaze. 'I *was* nervous. David…all those people…not to mention Freddy.'

'Forget Freddy for the moment. He's a parasite and a nuisance and will be sorted. As for David…he wants that bond and, whether you were cracking jokes or not, you were letting him in even if it may not have seemed that way to you.'

Sofia reddened and her eyes skittered away. How could he be so *nice*, so…*perceptive*…and yet at times so coolly remote?

'I'm not looking for a bond with anyone, least of all someone who's never been part of my life,' she tried, in the guise of a spirited argument to quell that side of her that seemed so foolishly susceptible to the glimpses she kept getting of a guy who could still get under her skin and stay there.

'Stop looking for an argument, Sofia. We're going to be...' his mouth quirked, and again that glimpse of humour that could thread past the defences she knew she should be mounting 'husband and wife for the foreseeable future. We need to get along...like husband and wife.' He tilted his head and looked levelly back at her.

'We'll be leading separate lives. That's what you said. We won't even be sharing the same space.'

He had the most incredible eyes. So deep and dark, glittering with a hard, steely edge that was somehow chilling and sinfully sexy at the same time.

'We will tonight.'

'Will what?'

'Be sharing the same space. We're going back to my place.'

'I don't want to do that.'

'Yes, you do.' He raised his eyebrows and stared at her. 'You drank quite a bit back there in the restaurant. Are you telling me that you fancy the thought of trekking back to the cottage?'

'You were paying attention to how much I drank?' Her stomach heaved and she breathed in deeply. *Inhale, exhale, inhale, exhale.*

'I'm your husband. Of course I was. Right now, I'd say you're looking a little green round the gills. How much did you eat?'

'Not a lot.' Sofia settled resentful green eyes on him but his crooked half-smile was disarming. 'What did you expect? I was sitting next to…next to…'

'You can say it.'

'Next to *David*. Eating and enjoying the food was the last thing on my mind.'

'You were nervous. Like I said. Hence my remark that you did well today. My godfather hasn't looked so energised in a while.'

'If he was energised, then it wasn't something I deliberately set out to achieve.'

'It's not the road you walk but the fact that you get there,' Rafael drawled. 'But back to you. You've barely eaten and you've probably drunk a lot more than you're accustomed to. Dispatching you back to the cottage to fend for yourself isn't on the cards. Besides…shouldn't the blushing bride spend the first night in the same county as her newly acquired husband at the very least?'

'Ha-ha, hilarious.' She rested her head back against the seat and closed her eyes for a few seconds. When she glanced sideways at him, it was to find his dark eyes resting on her face and she flushed.

She deliberately held her hand out and reminded herself that the ring on her finger was worth as much as she would have got in a year of dutiful nannying. *Business transaction*, she told herself. *Keep it real.*

'Very nice,' Rafael drawled, and he took her hand in his and looked at the ring, which made her heartily wish she hadn't drawn attention to it in the first place.

'All in a day's work,' she responded, quick as a flash, and he burst out laughing and dropped her hand.

It burned and tingled where he had briefly held it.

'You don't give in, do you, *cara*?' His eyes rested on her face. He was still grinning. 'A man could either be scared of that or turned on by it.'

Which are you? The question sizzled in her brain before she accepted that he was just teasing, playing a game, definitely *not flirting*.

'Can I ask you something?' Her voice was hurried and breathless in her eagerness to change the subject and escape the frantic tug of unwanted sensations flitting through her like quicksilver.

'Fire away.'

'You said you wanted to lead a single life, a *discreet* single life…so is there anyone waiting in the wings for you now that this marriage is out of the way?' She thought of the eager-to-please English roses and wondered if those were his type.

He looked momentarily staggered and she fuzzily thought, *Why the big show of ruffled feathers when you lied to me about who you really were and what you really wanted? Since when do liars have any right to look shocked at being asked whether they were having an affair with a married woman?* It felt strangely comforting to be antagonistic.

'Tell me that you're kidding?' Rafael exploded with incredulity.

'Why would I be kidding?' She shrugged and made to look away but he held her chin in his hand again and she shot him a sullen look from under her lashes.

'We're here,' he gritted, 'but this conversation isn't finished.'

His driver disappeared as seamlessly as he had appeared and they entered his sprawling place in silence. She could feel the simmering tension inside him and defiantly told herself that it was a perfectly reasonable question to have asked, given the circumstances of their relationship.

He slammed on lights and then spun around to look at her.

'Sorry,' Sofia said stiffly, keeping her distance, 'I don't know what made me ask that. None of my business, as I'm sure you'll rush in and point out, and if you don't mind I think

I'll go upstairs and go to sleep. Will I be in the same room as before?'

'Apology not accepted,' Rafael returned, standing with his arms folded, as immovable as the rock of Gibraltar and as menacing as a bouncer facing down a vagrant outside a posh night club.

'Actually, I don't feel too good.'

'Too bad.'

'I need to have some water. I need to sit down.'

'You can have a bottle of water and sit by all means, but you're going to tell me what the hell you meant by that.'

'Or else what?'

She looked at him and felt a slow burn as his dark eyes travelled from her mulish gaze to her parted lips.

'I just think I have a right to know who to steer clear of. Those women at the restaurant were stunning.' She ploughed on recklessly. 'Who knows if you're having fun with one of them?'

'They're wives of friends. Jesus, this is getting more unbelievable by the second.'

'Since when does that make a difference? I've had married men hit on me in the past.'

'Don't go there, Sofia…'

Suddenly the fight went out of her. Her stomach was back to churning and she could feel a headache coming on.

'I don't want to have this conversation, Rafael.' Her voice hitched and she stared down at the expensive shoes. 'I feel sick and tired and… overwhelmed…'

'You have an annoying habit of starting conversations you don't want to finish.' He raked his hands through his hair then, without warning and just as she was about to take a few tottering steps towards the kitchen, her mouth as dry as the desert, he covered the distance between them.

She froze, and then promptly un-froze when he scooped her up in one easy movement, carrying her towards the kitchen and kicking the door open with his foot while she wriggled and tried to disentangle herself.

'Keep still,' he warned.

'Put me down!'

'I intend to.'

He deposited her on one of the kitchen chairs and then stood back as she straightened herself with one shaking hand, barely able to meet his eyes.

'Why did you do that?' she asked accusingly.

'Because I got fed up having a long, going-nowhere conversation in my hall with you.' He turned and fetched her a glass of water. 'Drink this. You need to hydrate. Do you want something to eat?'

'Something like what?'

'God, you're the most difficult woman I have ever met in my entire life.'

'Well, *that* doesn't augur well for this marriage of ours!' Sofia couldn't contain her sarcasm and he suddenly grinned. Her pulse-rate accelerated into overdrive.

'Like I said, the one thing it ain't going to be is boring,' he murmured. 'Now, stop talking for five seconds and listen to me carefully. I don't have relationships with married women. Never. I don't care how many of them throw themselves at me and I don't care what they look like. A married woman is out of bounds.'

'But you would be happy to have an affair

with another woman even though *you're* married!' Sofia threw at him for the sake of argument, promptly forgetting all good intentions to keep things cool and civil between them without emotions of any sort getting in the way.

'As we both know, this isn't the real deal. If it were, then there is no way I would go near any woman. Believe it or not, I may have relationships but I like to stick to one woman at a time. You look sick. You need to go to bed.'

'I drank too much,' Sofia conceded. She stood up but her legs were suddenly wobbly and she had to stand still to gather herself for a few moments. She knew that he was looking at her, so cool, so urbane, so sophisticated. So much the opposite to her.

And just like that the tears she had been desperately trying to hold back began to leak out.

Horrified, she stared down at her feet and clenched her jaw.

'You're…crying. Are you *crying*, Sofia?'

Sofia shrugged. She didn't trust herself to speak but she heard him curse softly under his breath and then he was lifting her up again, as if sweeping her off her feet was becoming a habit, and this time she didn't bother to put up a fight.

She squeezed her eyes tightly shut. Her dress was riding up, exposing her thighs, but she couldn't be bothered to redress that by trying to tug it down.

Instead, she kept her eyes shut while he laid her very gently on the bed, then she immediately turned away and buried her head in the crook of her arms.

'Wait right there,' Rafael said gruffly. 'I'm going to bring up a jug of water and some tablets. And something to eat. You need to put food into your stomach. Don't move.'

How long was he gone?

She didn't know. She was aware of him putting the water on the table by the bed, and after a while she heard the sound of the door shutting quietly. When she peeped out, it was to find that an inelegantly enormous door-wedge of a sandwich had been made for her, which made her smile.

It was man fare, but it tasted wonderful.

And then, still feeling sick but so, so relieved to be in bed, she found herself drifting off.

The day she had been dreading was at an end. She would put all thoughts of her father on hold for the moment. She would definitely put all thoughts of Rafael on hold! Although, she felt herself smiling again at the sandwich he had made for her, stuffed full of cheese and ham but lacking everything else.

She fell asleep to the throbbing of a dull head-ache.

When she next opened her eyes, the room was pitch-black and it took her a few seconds to surface and remember exactly where she was.

In Rafael's house, with the duvet cover loosely draped over her, because she had obviously kicked it off at some point during the night.

Her half-closed eyes peeped from beneath the duvet but she was already registering what she wanted her startled eyes to confirm. The lilac dress had been removed, as had the shoes she'd been wearing when she had been deposited on the bed.

No bra! But then, she hadn't been wearing one. Her underwear, the lacy thong for her eyes only, was still there…

With a groan of horror, she began sitting up… and there he was, a dark shadow in a chair next to the bed.

He'd dragged over the chair by the dressing table and positioned it so that he could stretch out his long legs. His hands were linked loosely and his computer was on the ground next to him. She could see the dull flicker of the screen, which had gone into sleep mode.

Was he asleep? Awake? Something in the middle? He'd changed into a pair of jeans and a T-shirt.

She'd begun to sink back under the duvet when, as calmly as if he were continuing a conversation they'd only just been having, 'You're awake. How's the head?'

'What are you *doing* here?' She shuffled into an upright position, making sure that the duvet was tightly tucked around her, although she could feel the press of her bare breasts against the silky cotton.

'You were sick during the night.'

'I wasn't!' Had she been?

'Too much alcohol. Happens.'

'You took my dress off.'

'I took your dress off. One of us had to do it and it wasn't going to be you.'

'How could you?' she half-sobbed.

'Sofia, you were half-asleep and clawing at it because you were uncomfortable. No one can sleep in something that's as close-fitting as a second skin. You're probably embarrassed, but you don't have to be. You're not the first naked woman I've ever laid eyes on.'

Sofia drew her knees up to her chest and rested her head on them, wishing, more than anything else that he would just disappear—*poof*, like a genie heading back into the bottle where he belonged.

It was okay for him—so she was just another half-naked female body!—but it wasn't okay for *her*. This wasn't supposed to have happened.

'I've never felt so mortified in my entire life!' she all but wailed, then froze as he levered himself up and moved to sit on the bed right next to her.

'I didn't lay a finger on you,' Rafael said roughly. He shifted and she drew back.

'That's not the point. I wouldn't have expected you to. It's not as though you're attracted to me. But I just hate the thought of…of…'

'Not *attracted to you*?' Rafael laughed shortly. 'What ever gave you *that* idea? And you don't get to clam up on me this time and go into hiding because you're finding the conversation you started a little uncomfortable. Have you looked in a mirror recently, Sofia? Do you have any idea how sexy you are? Especially in a dress that was made to be torn off.'

'Made to be *torn off*?'

'I saw you walking towards me and I discovered what it felt like to forget how to breathe.'

'You don't mean that!'

'I was attracted to you the first time I ever set eyes on you.'

'You weren't, Rafael.' Her nerves were racing and she knew, *she knew*, that she shouldn't be having this conversation, because it was as dangerous as throwing a match onto tinder, but she couldn't help herself.

And she *liked it*. Liked hearing what he was saying.

'You went out to Argentina to check me out,

to see whether I would pass muster for the rich father I'd never met. You pretended...'

'Pretended that I was attracted to you? Hate to burst the bubble of self-righteous hostility, Sofia, but I'm not that good an actor.'

Sofia could barely breathe. She was spellbound by the intense glitter in his dark eyes, mesmerised by his softly spoken words. She didn't know whether he was saying stuff he wanted her to hear, but why would he do that? What would be the point?

'You made sure to tell me that this wasn't a real relationship,' she pointed out accusingly. 'You made sure to let me know that you intended to be off doing your own thing while I pottered and did whatever I fancied doing for a year, buried in a cottage in the countryside.'

'Think that was because I didn't want you in my bed?' He leapt to his feet, leaving a cold, empty space next to her on the bed. She watched as he restlessly paced the room when the only thing she wanted was for him to return to the bed. Her head was as clear as a bell but the darkness gave her courage to say what was on her mind. She felt a surge of reckless, heady daring. When she thought about what he'd said, everything inside her melted.

Eyes wide, she followed his jerky progress through the room. When he finally came to stand in front of her, she didn't huddle into a defensive ball. Instead, she stared right back up at him with a degree of boldness she hadn't known she possessed.

So he fancied her. So she hadn't been the only one to feel that fierce, uncontrollable attraction.

'What else was I supposed to think?'

'This conversation is…' He shook his head and looked away for a few seconds, but his eyes swerved back to her upturned face.

'Is what?'

'Dangerous,' Rafael said softly.

'Okay.'

'*Okay?* Is that all you have to say on the matter?'

'I feel better about you taking the dress off.'

'Because you wanted it off or because you now know that you turn me on?' He didn't take his eyes off her when he said that.

Heat crawled through her. She felt the pinch of her nipples and a spreading dampness between her thighs. She'd never wanted anyone as much as she wanted him, right here and right now. But she just didn't have it in her to take that final step and brazenly invite him into bed with her.

'I don't know,' she whispered.

'Sofia, I made a conscious decision not to do anything about the attraction I felt for you because I didn't want to complicate an already complicated situation.'

'What do you mean?'

'What do you think I mean? I wanted this to be about business. Emotions have a way of stealing the show and never in a good way.'

'My emotions or yours?'

'I don't have emotions.'

Sofia opened her mouth to tell him that he surely didn't mean that but then realised that he really did. Or that was what he told himself, because when she thought about how devoted he was to his godfather she knew that he was far from being the unemotional hard case he purported to be.

So what did they have here? Stripped down to the bare bones, what they had was a physical attraction that was as strong as a riptide, as darkly powerful as the swirl of a dangerous whirlpool in the middle of still waters.

'Nor do I,' she said boldly. 'Not for you, at any rate.'

'What are you trying to tell me, *cara*?' Rafael asked thickly.

'I'm trying to tell you that I wish you'd come sit on the bed again.'

Rafael looked at her for a long moment and she wondered whether, having reached a crossroads, he would now turn his back and walk away, stick to following his head.

She'd come so close to opening herself up to him physically when they had been out in Argentina before the truth had spilled out. She was at that point again, all cards on the table.

He slowly moved towards her and she felt her breathing slow as she watched him. So beautiful, so graceful, so mesmerisingly alpha male.

Her eyes tracked a leisurely route from face to torso and then down to where his jeans pulled tightly across his thighs.

'You're playing with fire,' he said shakily, but his hand was resting lightly on the zipper of his trousers and she stared, fascinated, as he undid it.

She didn't want to give herself time to think or even to remember that this was not the sort of thing she'd ever done before. She didn't want her head to start following his lead and take control of the situation.

She didn't want her own negative experiences in the past to determine what happened at this precise moment in time.

'Maybe I am,' she agreed in a low voice. 'I've never played with fire before.'

'Never?' He smiled, lowered himself next to her on the bed and stretched out, arms folded behind his head. Sofia remained upright but shifted so that she was looking down at him. His gaze slid across to her and stayed there.

'No. Have you?'

'Once. Doesn't everyone need a learning curve? Let me see you.'

'See me?'

'You know what I mean.' He trailed a finger along her collar bone, beneath which the duvet was still pulled up tightly, shielding her naked breasts.

She slowly let the duvet drop and watched with increasingly heated excitement as Rafael sat up, barely breathing, eyes trained on her nakedness.

Her nipples were pink and swollen and she released a long sigh, relaxing her whole body into his caress as he manoeuvred himself into a position from which he could take one bud into his mouth and gently suck on it.

He propelled her back so that she was lying flat, then pinned her hands above her head and straddled her.

'You have no idea how much you turn me on,' Rafael offered huskily. 'Everything about the way you look is a turn-on. The second I laid eyes on you, every other woman on the face of the earth faded into insignificance.'

Sweet words, she thought helplessly, *but so meaningless in the context of what we have. But what's the point of analysing? When we're bound together through convenience and destined to part company before the ink on the marriage certificate has time to dry?*

Meaningful or meaningless…did either matter when the physical need he aroused was so explosive?

She turned him on and that thought was as powerful as a rush of pure adrenaline...

She moved sinuously against the sheet and felt a rush of feminine empowerment as his nostrils flared and his eyes darkened in the grip of lust.

When he straightened to sling his legs over the side of the bed, he left behind a cool void that made her want to touch herself.

Should she tell him that she was not going to be able to live up to all those racy model types he dated? She'd known from the minute she'd begun developing what it felt like to have boys drool over her. Her first girlish crush had been a mistake, and her experiences after that had rammed home to her that the only reason men looked twice at her was because of her appearance. She hadn't asked to be born sexy, but she had been, and she had grown wary over the years. So wary that the touching and experimentation that should have been part and parcel of entering adulthood had passed her by.

The constant travel hadn't helped matters either.

Now, here she was, and he was in for a shock if he expected high jinks between the sheets.

Caught up in her thoughts, she gasped when she realised the T-shirt had been removed and the jeans were being dispatched to join it on the ground.

The bulge of his erection distorting the shape of his boxers brought hectic colour to her cheeks and she went as stiff as a board as he joined her on the bed under the duvet, pulling it up so that it covered both of them, drawing her close so that her breasts were squashed against his chest.

He slipped his hand between her thighs and stroked her softly, then he inserted his fingers underneath the damp underwear so that he could play with her.

The casual intimacy shocked her and her breathing was fast and hard as she stilled his hand.

'What is it?' Rafael drew back to stare at her, his expression only just discernible in the shadows. 'I know this is maybe a little unexpected for the both of us…something we hadn't catered for…'

'That's not it,' she whispered.

'Then what is?' His voice gentled but there was bemusement there as well. 'Talk to me, Sofia. Tell me.'

She gently touched his arm he cupped her face in one hand, looking right back at her with a deep, unwavering look.

'One minute you're hot and ready for me, and the next minute you're playing the shrinking virgin and pushing me away. What's that about? You don't play games…but is that what you're doing now, *cara*?'

He sounded genuinely bewildered and the reaction was so much the reaction of a decent guy that she felt something melt inside her.

'No games. But the shrinking virgin?' She breathed in deeply and went for it in a rush. 'What if I were to tell you that you're spot-on with that?'

'I'm not following you.' He drew back, frowning, and she could see that he was trying to join the dots and not getting there, because he just couldn't comprehend that a woman in her mid-twenties could still be a virgin.

In his world, racy models probably lost their virginity before their teens were up.

'I haven't…done this before, Rafael.'

'You…you must have.'

'Because I look the way I do? Do you judge all women by the way they look?'

Rafael flushed darkly but remained silent.

'You're a contradiction,' he mused slowly. 'I sensed that from the very first. You're fiery and outspoken but there's something strangely tentative about you. How? How is it that you never slept with a man?'

Sofia shrugged. She suddenly felt vulnerable, on the verge of giving something of herself away, yet he was only asking her a question and expressing very understandable curiosity.

'You said that everyone has a learning curve,' she reminded him. 'I lost my heart when I was young to a good-looking guy. Turned out he and his mates had made a bet—to see whether he could get me into bed, because they all thought I was frigid.' She laughed mirthlessly. 'I guess I became vigilant when it came to the opposite sex, careful not to let anyone in, because the last thing I needed was to get hurt all over again. Time moved on... We kept changing post codes because my mother was all over the place when it came to guys, so the opportunity never arose...and there you have it.'

'Parents have a lot to answer for,' Rafael thought aloud, his tone so low and sincere that she stopped worrying about closely held confidences.

'I just wanted you to know,' she said helplessly.

'And now I do.'

CHAPTER SEVEN

A VIRGIN. IT beggared belief that the sexiest woman he had ever laid eyes on was *a virgin*. And yet, thinking about it, it certainly explained all those intangible contradictions he had subliminally observed in her.

He stared at her and the glass-green eyes staring back at him conveyed a mixture of challenge and hesitation that cut right to the core of him. He had never slept with a virgin and had never actually thought about what it might be like to sleep with one. Some men fantasised about that kind of thing. He wasn't one of them. He had lost his own virginity at a young age to an experienced older woman and he'd never looked back.

But now…

Something weirdly gentle and protective twisted inside him, a softness that he couldn't remember having experienced before.

'I would understand if you decided that a virgin wasn't what you had banked on.'

'Don't say that, *cara*.' He stroked her face, touching her as gently as someone would touch a piece of priceless china. So tough, so strong and yet so damned fragile. 'Sofia, I should be the one asking you whether you want to go ahead with this. I'm not Mr Right. I don't do love. I...' Rafael hesitated. 'I've seen where love goes and it's...what can I say?...never to a good place. David is a case in point. Two ridiculous marriages to women who bled him dry...and of course his relationship with your mother that came to nothing.'

Not to mention his own parents, Sofia thought, sinking into the tenderness that had sprung up between them, of which he was probably unaware. Tenderness wouldn't be an emotion factored into his psyche and he was oh, so entrenched in the notion that he could control every aspect of his life, including every single emotion. He'd said that parents had a lot to answer for and she knew, whether he was capable of voicing it himself or not, that he had lived through the dark side of love, the all-consum-

ing love of two people who had had no time for
the son they had created because they'd been
too selfish, too self-indulgent. All round, his
experiences would have left a bitter taste in his
mouth and soured his vision of what could be
a wonderful thing.

Had he any idea how...*human*...those very
things made him?

'No,' she whispered, pulling him towards her,
breathing in the clean scent of whatever after-
shave he was wearing. 'You're not Mr Right,
but you're the only guy I want just at this moment in time and I don't want to look beyond
that. I just want to...enjoy myself and go with
the flow and not think about what's right or
what's wrong...'

His nakedness stilled her. Undressed, he was
everything she had imagined him to be and
much, much more. She stared at his impressive size and wondered at the technicalities of
what happened next.

But he knew she was a virgin and he hadn't
backed off. The very opposite.

'Don't be nervous,' he soothed, settling next

to her and flipping her so that they were stom-ach to stomach, looking at one another in the darkness of the bedroom. 'I'll be gentle. When it comes to sex, you'd be surprised. I can have a very slow hand. I'll take care of you.'

Now, he guided her hand to touch him and continued talking to her in a low, seductive voice while he showed her how to excite him.

'Not too fast and not too hard.' He licked her ear and nuzzled against her neck while she squirmed wetly in the panties that had yet to be removed and banked down the urge to push him against her breasts, which ached. Would that be too forward?

He kept his hand over hers, moving it slowly, firmly, guiding her until she was losing herself in the sensation of feeling his arousal.

Then he deftly removed her panties, slipping them down and gently inserting his hand be-tween her thighs.

He rested the palm of his hand over her and it felt so good that she parted her legs, encour-aging him to do more, but he didn't and that stoked the urgent excitement inside her until she wanted to scream with frustration.

She whimpered when he removed his hand so that he could explore the rest of her body.

He kissed her, a long, lingering kiss, tongues meshing, breathing into her mouth and filling her with suffocating longing. He nuzzled the side of her neck, sweeping her long hair back and sifting his fingers through its length. He took his time paying attention to her breasts, circling one swollen nipple with his mouth and suckling on it while he toyed with the other with his fingers, gently rubbing and rousing until the whimpers turned into moans of barely contained excitement.

She squirmed against his mouth and pressed his head so that the caress deepened, deepened until darts of erotic pleasure were shooting through her body, from her toes to the very tips of her fingers. He smoothed his hand over her flat belly, tracing each curve and indent, from the dip of her waist to the soft oval of her belly button. And then this time, when he felt the dampness between her legs, he didn't just let the flat of his hand cup her. He deftly inserted his finger, instantly finding her sensitive clitoris, and she gasped, eyes opening, as he began stroking.

It didn't take long. She'd never come close to this level of sensation and she came fast, unable to contain the rising surge of pleasure as he continued to stroke, his movements firm and rhythmic.

She arched back with a low shuddering groan and her eyes fluttered shut as she reached her orgasm against his finger.

She subsided, pink-faced and dismayed.

'I'm sorry.'

'What for?'

'Rafael…'

'Shh…trust me.' He caressed her lightly, taking his time, and his mouth replaced his fingers. He licked a trail along her breasts down to her belly button and then he took his time, teasing the soft inside of her thighs.

Having crested one explosive wave of sensation, Sofia didn't think that it would be possible to do anything more than just flop like a rag doll in the aftermath, but she was wrong.

Her body slowly awakened. She moved against him, desperate to pleasure him the way he had pleasured her, shyly wondering whether she would be any good.

She was mystified as to how she could ever have relegated sex to the position of second-rate companion to the bigger thing called *love*. She'd imagined herself meeting the perfect guy, someone kind and gentle, and her imagination had stopped at the bedroom door.

Rafael wasn't the perfect guy, and he didn't even bother to try and pretend otherwise. He'd entered into a contract with her, and then it had been a case of, 'oh, by the way, I fancy you so why not?', but that was where personal involvement had ended, even though in some strange way she didn't feel *used*. They talked. Was that it? They laughed together. Okay, so they might not have a romantic connection, and he might scoff at all talk of anything more than sex and lust, but they *communicated*. She wondered whether that was why she could give herself to him the way she was doing now.

He'd kicked that bedroom door open and was showing her just how inadequate all her fuzzy daydreams had been—showing her that there was no such thing as black and white when it came to the physical side of a relationship.

The reality of his strong, lean, naked body against hers was explosive. She wriggled as he nudged his sensuous path downwards and then breathed in sharply as his mouth pressed softly against her womanhood, nuzzling the downy fur between her legs, then inserting his tongue into the slick groove and licking her.

She couldn't breathe.

Time stood still. Little shivers raced through her body, darting here, there and everywhere. She could feel pleasure building, and he could sense it as well, because he drew back, briefly enough for her to want just a little bit more.

The stop-start teasing was driving her crazy. He took her almost to the brink, only to bring her back down again, and in the end she was the one to tell him that she was ready.

'I want you in me,' she urged with wicked abandon, tugging him up by the hair and writhing as he wrapped his arm around her.

She had been apprehensive about the pain but she needn't have worried. He'd promised to be gentle and he was. He fumbled over the condom, which made her smile, but when he settled back into her she was ready for him, slick and wet, and she felt just the smallest discomfort when he began to thrust more firmly into her.

'Relax, *cara*,' he urged. 'I'm going as slowly as I can but it's hard. You're driving me crazy and all I want is to move inside you.'

'I want that too, Rafael.' It was a struggle to talk because after the discomfort her body began to respond in ways she couldn't have predicted, soaring and swooping as, encouraged by her, he started thrusting with more force and purpose.

His bigness filled her up and carried her away until she lost touch with everything around her and the world was reduced to sensation.

She came with shuddering force, crying out, nails digging into his back, legs drawn up as he plunged deeply to find his own orgasm.

Sated, they remained locked together for a few minutes, then he rolled off her and stared up at the ceiling.

She wanted to talk. She felt an intense intimacy and she would have loved nothing more than to curl against him, have him stroke her and chat, laugh and cuddle.

It was a cool reminder of what this was all about when he slid off the bed and headed straight to the *en suite* bathroom, shutting the door behind him.

With the ardour fast draining out of her, Sofia remained where she was. She had just shared the most wonderful and earth-shattering experience of her entire life but had it been the same for him? Dared she hope?

She should protect herself—should remind herself that, for Rafael, this had been just a physical act. But she was weakly conscious of her thoughts and feelings all over the place, as though she'd been thrown into a tumble dryer and spun at high speed until nothing was quite where it should have been. She wondered whether he was disappointed with her performance and tried hard not to care, instead forcing her way through the drowsy contentment, trying to settle to reach a place where she could, at least, face him with a certain amount of self-control.

She sat up, drawing the duvet right up to

her neck. With the bathroom light on behind him, he was a shadowy figure, hovering, and she watched him for a few moments, not quite knowing where they went from here.

'Are you…finished in there? I thought I might have a shower.'

Rafael slowly towards her and then sat at the side of the bed, depressing it with his weight.

Her hands itched to reach out and touch him, pull him back to her, but her natural caution had kicked in and she looked at him warily, wondering what was going through his head.

'That was—' he began, and she interrupted before he could say something that would unintentionally hurt her.

'I know. Probably not the best for you…' She laughed nervously and his eyes narrowed.

'I was going to say…that was incredible.'

Happiness bloomed inside her. 'I got the impression that you couldn't wait to hop out of bed.'

'I wanted to take you again and I knew I couldn't in case you were…sore. Or just needed some time out. It was safer for me to have a shower and get my act together.'

Sofia smiled shyly and touched his chest with her fingers, lightly circling his flat, brown nipple and enjoying the way his breathing thickened in response.

He caught her hand and then absently stroked her fingers with his thumb, eyes pinned to her face.

'I could commute,' he murmured thoughtfully.

'Meaning?'

His voice was soft. 'Meaning that I enjoyed that and I'd quite like to carry on enjoying it.'

'That wasn't part of the plan.'

'Plans can change.'

'You didn't want complications.'

'Does it have to be get complicated?' He tilted his head to one side. 'We both know what this situation is all about, and there's a time line, which in all probability will be less than the allotted year. In the meantime…we're married and all we're doing is what all married people do.' He looked at her, gaze serious. 'We're enjoying some hot sex before it all starts to unravel. The only difference is that we have the advantage of not being ambushed by disappointment when the inevitable happens.'

Faced with this stark choice, Sofia knew that she either indulged a sexual curiosity she'd never known she possessed, and for the foreseeable future sacrifice her principles about saving herself for the right guy to come along, or she walked away. But when she thought about walking away she was gripped with an emptiness so intense that she wanted to howl.

'You're right.' She decided on the spot and met that serious gaze with equal gravity. 'We both know the score. What's to get complicated?'

Sofia approached the door to the opulent sitting room in her father's house with her usual trepidation.

Old habits died hard, and even though it had been several weeks since the wedding, and even though she had seen him several times since then, she was still to shed her stiffness when she was around him.

Rafael oiled the wheels by always being present, allowing her to watch and contribute when she wanted to from a safe distance, but this time there was no Rafael.

'Running late,' he had phoned to say just as she had been stepping out of the Mercedes that had delivered her to the house. 'I'll be there as soon as I can, but this meeting has overrun and I can't walk out. I'm discovering all sorts of mess created by David's damned stepson. Some through sheer incompetence, but some needs delving into because I'm getting a whiff of things not as they should be. No idea what exactly is being concealed but I intend to find out and take him to the cleaners.'

What could she say? She knew the boundaries to what they had and she wasn't going to overstep them. They had great sex. They came together in bed and were the perfect fit. It was a situation that wasn't going anywhere and she knew that. Rafael didn't have to repeat the mantra about theirs being a marriage of convenience, with a time limit as to its duration. That was a given, and she accepted it because what she got in return was mind-blowing.

How could sex be *so good*?

And out of bed…

She was learning how to make her way around him, how to manage him. Never had she met someone so dominant, so hard-wired to get his own way. No wonder he hadn't batted an eyelid when it had been a case of hunting her down in Argentina and checking her out. He adored his godfather and he had brought one hundred percent of his incredible focus to doing what he had been asked to do. That she might have been hurt had not really occurred to him. Collateral damage was just something that happened. He was complex, infuriating, yet wonderfully exhilarating all at the same time, and Sofia knew that she was getting more and more sucked into his powerful aura with each passing day.

She didn't like to think about time slipping past. The fact that he wasn't standing here right now, in front of the imposing front door to her father's exquisite Belgravia house, was a reminder of how much she had come to depend on the support he gave her without even realising that she was doing so.

Not just support when it came to interacting with her father but support with the accountancy course she had been determined to pursue, support with the landscaping of the garden to the cottage they visited on the weekends, dismissing what he didn't like with a casual wave of his hand, and reminding her of how little interest he had in anything outdoors and green, yet glancing at the pictures she showed him and expressing opinions with his typical self-assurance. There were times when he slung his arm over her shoulders and leant into her to say something, and she could almost forget that what they had wasn't actually *real*.

She rang the doorbell and, as soon as her father greeted her, she knew that he was well aware that his godson wasn't going to be there.

'Nice to have you to myself!' David beamed, ignoring her tight, apprehensive expression and spinning round to lead the way into the sitting room, where tea was always taken. A part of her unexpectedly softened because his tenacity when it came to building a bond with her was slowly cutting through her defences.

Over the weeks, he had gained weight and was fond of dismissing the dietary guidelines strictly laid down by the nurse 'companion' he had hired to cook for him and oversee all his physical requirements, including distributing his tablets, which he had no trouble forgetting to take.

He was talking about nothing in particular, asking her about what she had been up to, and she found herself chatting back.

'For a fake marriage,' he mused, depositing himself on one of the deep chairs, 'You seem to have some pretty real headaches. Rafael's selfish, my dear. It's a learned skill.'

Sofia scowled and wondered how she'd managed to blather on so much about him that David had actually picked up on it. She opened her mouth to protest and found herself asking with a nonchalant toss of her head, 'What do you mean that it's a learned skill? How can someone learn to be selfish? Not that I'm concerned one way or the other.'

Their eyes met, and she blushed.

'He had to learn how to be a man when he was just a boy,' David mused thoughtfully. 'By which I mean that he had to learn how to suffer disappointment and rise above it.'

'Because his parents weren't around?' What was wrong with a little curiosity?

'Because they were very fond of making promises about visiting and then failing to deliver on the day because something better had come up. By the time Rafael was ten, he'd learned that waiting by the window of his dorm was pretty much a waste of time. So you see, my dear, independence was thrust upon him and selfishness became a way of life, because if you didn't think about anyone else you couldn't be hurt.'

Sofia's eyes pricked. This was the first real conversation she had had with her father, because Rafael wasn't around, and a warmth spread through her that fought through her stubborn pride. She blinked, cleared her throat and changed the subject but her head was full of images of a disappointed child wondering why his parents hadn't shown up for the Nativity play or Sports Day or whatever else kids at posh boarding schools did with their free time.

'The old bag has gone the extra mile and made some tasty little treats for us.' He was waving his hand at the highly polished sideboard which was laden with exquisite titbits—delicate sandwiches, blinis and an assortment of miniature cakes.

'I say *made*. She unbent enough to make the sandwiches, and those funny little things there, but told me that if I wanted more I'd have to hire someone else. The cheek! Good job I'm just the sort of understanding employer she can't tear herself away from!' He chuckled, peering at the array and filling his plate while Sofia shot to her feet and gently removed the plate.

'You can't eat most of this stuff,' she chided.

'The old witch isn't around to supervise. Gave her a few hours off. Didn't want her hovering and glowering.'

'Gladys is one of the nicest people I have ever met.'

'Hmph. Got the kind of thing I thought you'd enjoy, my dear. Your mother always had a soft spot for pastries. Used to enjoy watching her eat them. Delicate as a cat, licking her fingers one by one.'

Sofia stilled because this was one of those

rare occasions when her mother had been mentioned.

Blushing furiously, she helped herself to what was on offer, very much aware of her father using a walker to return to his favourite chair, chatting about this and that, telling her about all the amazing changes Rafael had already initiated in the company.

It left her with a burning desire to bring the conversation back round to her mother but not quite knowing how she could achieve that.

So much the coward, she thought…too scared to let go of past resentments yet too scared to confront them.

'You were talking about my mother.' She interrupted him mid-sentence, before immediately frowning down at her half-empty china plate. She had poured them both cups of tea and hastily she gulped a hot mouthful, then darted a look at David to find him staring thoughtfully back at her.

'Not if it upsets you, my dear,' he said gently. 'And I know it does. You don't enjoy raking over the past any more than I do and I apologise if I inadvertently said anything to upset you.'

'You haven't.' She was beetroot-red, but now that she had embarked on this she couldn't jump ship. 'I… I *want* to talk about it. It's been festering inside me and I want to know why you dumped my mum. You and Rafael think that I can just shove the past away into a box and pretend it never happened, but she was never the same after you walked out on her. She was… she *became*…a mess as time went by.' She looked away but it was taking everything she had inside her not to start crying.

She cringed as he heaved himself out of the deep chair using his walker, and made the few steps towards her, sinking onto the blue velvet sofa and patting the side for her to join him.

'My dear, I have no idea what you're talking about,' he said, bewildered. 'I never dumped your mother. It was the other way around!'

'That's not true,' she whispered.

'You have to listen to me, Sofia. I was called away on urgent family business all those years ago. A life-and-death situation that left me no time to contact your mother, so I left word with a friend and colleague, the only one who knew the details of our relationship in its entirety. I told him to explain to your mother what had happened. I left a letter, all sorts of forwarding details. Told him to tell her that I would be back, that she must wait. I had the ring, my dear. I had dreams.'

Sofia stared. 'But—but that can't be right,' she stammered. 'No, you have to be lying... mistaken...'

'I kept the ring. I have it. I never put it on the finger of the woman I stupidly married because I was hurting. I still look at that ring.'

'But you dumped her... Jon James told her that you couldn't face telling her yourself but it was over. He told her to leave the hotel immediately before it became a public scandal. He said that there would be no references if the whole truth came out. She left and never looked back.'

The silence settled over them.

Restless in her own skin and thoughts all over the place, Sofia was dimly aware that she was asking questions, and lots of them, voice jerky and shaking as she pieced together a tale of a jealous colleague who had lied to both parties because the woman he wanted, her mother, had rejected his advances. Jon James, it turned out, was long gone but he had left behind a legacy that had outlived him because he had played with the truth and told enough lies with sufficient conviction to make sure he destroyed what could have been.

As proof of David's unrequited love, she was eventually shown the ring her father had bought for the woman he had intended to marry. It was ornate, engraved, and her mother would have loved it. She'd always had a soft spot for the garish.

Sofia stared at it for such a long time that she felt as though she was freezing on the spot.

'I should go,' she said, eventually. When she looked at him she saw the man she had slowly been accepting over time—a strong, kind man who would have made her mother happy.

'I want you to have the ring,' David said. 'It was only ever mine on loan, waiting for its rightful owner, and that rightful owner should now be you.'

'But I already have a ring. And, besides, this is a marriage in name only…'

'Then hang on to it, my dear, until the real

thing happens. All these misunderstandings… a terrible waste, a terrible shame, and yet to know that I was loved. It's a comfort, just as it would be a comfort for you to take what was destined for your dear mother.'

In the dim recesses of her brain, Sofia felt that she should want to telephone her aunt immediately and share this tumultuous development, but the person who beckoned to her as confidante was Rafael, and she was waiting for him when he returned to his apartment a scant half-hour after she had arrived back.

He paused in the doorway and her heart leapt in her chest as she stared at him, drinking in the lean lines of his body and that oddly endearing state of semi-dishevelment in which he returned every evening: tie off, shirt cuffed to the elbows, staging a war against the waistband of his handmade trousers, black hair tousled.

'You're back.' He looked at her narrowly while absently hanging his tie over the banister.

'It's been…it's been draining,' Sofia whispered, moving towards him and not caring what he thought as she stepped into his arms. After just the briefest of hesitations, he wrapped his arms around her and breathed into her hair.

'Tell me.'

'I feel terrible,' she all but sobbed when she had recounted every detail of the afternoon, leaving nothing out. Somehow, without letting her go, they had worked their way to the kitchen and he broke apart to pour her a small amount of brandy in a goblet.

'Drink this,' he urged. 'You've had a traumatic afternoon and there's nothing better for a bout of trauma than a swig of brandy.'

'I don't want you to let me go,' Sofia confessed in a raw undertone, creeping back into his arms and sipping some of the fiery liquid before setting the glass down on the kitchen counter.

She didn't care what he thought of that statement. She just knew that his arms around her filled her with a sense of well-being and a feeling of *rightness*.

This was where she belonged, she thought wonderingly. Just like that, her mind flashed back to all the times they had spent in one another's company. She had summed it all up as two people uniting between the sheets but now she recalled the conversations they had had, the laughter they had shared, and now this...

Wanting him and only him at a time when she had needed soothing.

She loved him and she didn't know how that had happened or when. She just knew that all her thoughts were of him. He was in her head from the moment she opened her eyes to the second she closed them, and she couldn't imagine a time when he might not be there. David had said to hold on to the ring for a time when the *real* marriage happened. What a joke!

Could he ever love her? It happened, didn't it? People got accustomed to someone and love crept up and ambushed them, wiped out all their cynicism, took them by surprise...

She would never tell him how she felt because she knew that he'd run a mile.

But there were other ways of reminding him that she was a part of his life and perhaps more invaluable than he might ever have expected.

'Let's go upstairs,' he murmured.

'I should cook us something to eat. I wouldn't mind some comfort food. I don't want any of that fancy stuff we order in from those restaurants.'

But she was winding her arms around his neck and stretching up to kiss him.

He adored her breasts and never stopped telling her.

She stepped back and kept her eyes locked to his as she slowly removed the shirt and flung it on the kitchen table, then the bra followed, releasing her heavy breasts.

His nostrils flared and his eyes darkened and a thrill of feminine power soared inside her.

With deliberate provocation, she held both her breasts in her hands and then, maintaining eye contact, she rotated the pads of her thumbs over the stiffened tips of her big nipples.

Rafael swore under his breath and when he spoke his voice was shaky.

'It's going to be a challenge making it up the stairs.'

'Then we'd better stay down here.'

He smiled slowly and now it was his turn to get undressed, starting with his belt, which he pulled free in one easy move. Then the trousers were down and he stepped out of them, revealing the blatant push of his formidable erection against his boxers.

Sofia stepped forward, dipped her hands under and took his stiffened member so that she could start teasing it, rolling it the way she knew he liked, slowly and firmly, feeling the steady pulsing beneath her fingers.

'Witch,' he growled in response, propelling her back until her rear nudged the edge of the kitchen table. And then, in a flurry of discarded clothes, and with an urgency that barely allowed him time to don the necessary protection, he was taking her.

He had her on the table with her legs around his waist, standing in front of her. When he thrust, pushing her back, the pleasure was so exquisite that she cried out and clutched him. He held her in place and kept thrusting, his bigness filling her up, sending her body into a shrieking, uncontrolled response. The only sounds were their breathing, moaning and grunting and she felt her wetness around him as he rammed harder inside her.

They came together, bodies slick with perspiration, tensing, stiffening and then, at last, coming down from the peaks of their mutual ecstasy.

For Sofia, this was love, and she never wanted it to end. Ever.

CHAPTER EIGHT

'I THINK I'D like to see…the company.' Sofia was stretched out on the bed, her hair spilling across the pillow, watching as Rafael got dressed to leave for work. She caught his eye in the reflection of the mirror as he adjusted his tie.

Despite his confidence that the annoying *Freddy situation* would be sorted within weeks, her father's stepson was still a thorn in Rafael's side and it was frustrating the hell out of him.

His level of incompetence was astounding, as he had confided only days previously, but the way he arrogantly strode through the office made it difficult for anyone to take issue with him.

Rafael was now involved in the painstaking process of trying to unpick some of the more stupid decisions Freddy had taken and somehow managed to get past the board of directors, primarily because of his process of dispatching the ones who might have stood in his way.

The whole process was taking Rafael away from his own responsibilities, handling his own sprawling empire, and he was fast losing patience.

'Why?' He swung round to look at her and she leapt out of bed, scooping up clothes along the way and heading towards the *en suite* bathroom.

'Do I have to have a reason?' she paused to ask him and he raised his eyebrows and dealt her a crooked smile.

'You don't have to,' he drawled, 'but I'm curious as to why. I didn't think you were interested in the company.'

'I wasn't but…it's been a few weeks since all that business with my mother emerged and ever since…well… I feel closer to him. We chat on the phone. He texts often. Have I told you that he's teaching me how to play chess?' She gazed at Rafael. By now, she could recreate every line on his beautiful face, every ingrained habit he wasn't even aware he had. 'And that's why I'm suddenly interested in seeing what goes on there. Will you wait for me while I have a shower? I won't be long.'

'Want me to join you?' His voice deepened and he moved an inch closer to her.

'I think I can manage a shower on my own, Rafael.' She placed her flattened palm against his chest. The slightest encouragement and he would whip off the hand-made suit, the silk tie and the pristine white shirt with the discreetly embroidered initials on the cuffs, and he would join her in the shower and they would make love again.

'Sure?' He covered her hand with his and tugged her towards him. 'You told me that you loved me soaping you...something about the thorough way I did it...'

'Honestly!' But she laughed, blushing furiously. He was shameless when it came to saying exactly what was on his mind. The things he whispered into her ear when they made love made her ears burn in the light of day.

'I adore the way you blush, *cara.*' His eyes were serious and he stroked her hair away from her face. 'Sweet and innocent, even though you set the sheets alight with your passion.'

For a second their eyes tangled and she felt that familiar thudding in her heart, as though they had merged, become one in a moment of unity that went far, far beyond the physical.

He was the first to draw back, frowning as though suddenly perplexed, suddenly at odds with whatever was going through his head.

'I'll get changed. I'll be quick. Time is money, as you once said.'

'I hate it when you quote me back to myself.' But he was smiling, relaxed, back to his usual self.

Twenty minutes later she emerged from a quick shower to find that he had already left the bedroom, and when she went downstairs there he was, waiting for her in the kitchen. He looked up from whatever he had been doing on his computer when she walked in.

'Sofia the businesswoman,' he murmured, standing and snapping shut the computer. 'I like it. Do you think I could be the sort of guy who enjoys a woman in a uniform? Or maybe I'm turned on by the buttoned-up-to-the neck look...'

She had twisted her long hair into a bun and

was wearing a white blouse, a pair of navy trousers and a jacket. Separately, each item was okay. As an ensemble, Rafael was right in that it screamed 'office'.

'Maybe I'm Sofia the accountant in the making,' she said lightly, leading the way out of the kitchen and waiting for him by the car.

'I've never known an accountant as sexy as you.' He opened the passenger door for her and then swung around to the driver's side but, before he started the engine, he turned to look at her. 'I'm glad you're coming,' he said seriously. 'You're right. David's headquarters is a part of him and, yes, a part you should see. He would be delighted.'

Pleasure bloomed inside her, and for a second she was lost for words, caught up in that side of him that could be incredibly gentle and incredibly perceptive. If she were to say how she felt, though, she knew that he would laugh, teasing her away from a place that could become too serious too fast. She'd learned how to manage him, had learned how to steer clear of places she knew he wouldn't want to visit.

'I thought I'd surprise him—tell him when I next see him.'

'Nice touch.'

Sofia looked at his arrogant, beautiful profile and wondered how she had ended up in this mess, wanting what was out of reach, hoping to get it just right so that she could grasp what her heart craved, always wondering whether that would ever be possible.

The question had barely been posed before the answer rose to the surface. She'd overestimated her ability to separate sex from love. She had assumed herself clever and cool enough to deal with a man who was leagues ahead of her in the sophistication stakes. She'd idiotically thought that she'd learnt all the lessons she needed to learn from the experiences of her mother and was therefore well equipped to withstand *anything*.

Now here she was, hoping that some of what she felt might eventually be returned in kind, while the clock ticked, time passed and the year they had set began to ebb away, like sand sifting through an hourglass.

When that year was up, she could of course

tell him that she wasn't ready to quit the marriage but she cringed to think that by then *he* might be ready to quit what they'd started, having accomplished what he had set out to achieve. Her relationship with David was thawing by the day, as she came to realise just how much he had loved her mother and just how keen he was to get to know her. And as for Freddy... That business would surely be sorted one way or another and, if not, if it was just destined to be an ongoing problem on which Rafael would have to permanently keep an eye, then it was still a pretty good trade-off for all the bits of the company that had been signed over to him and for the happiness David derived from knowing that the problem was being dealt with.

By the time their year was up, he would probably have packed her cases and changed the lock on the door.

'I'm just curious,' she said eventually. 'David has talked so much about how he started with the hotel business and I guess, yes, it's another facet to him that I'm keen to learn about. I'm not about to wade in and try sorting out the accounts department, so no need to worry about that!'

'Why would that be a worry for me?'

'Oh, I don't know,' Sofia said lightly. 'Maybe because I get the feeling that my role is to commute between London and the countryside and do not much of anything because I don't have to?'

'Have I ever said that?'

'No, but...'

'You're free to do whatever you want, Sofia. I don't own you, despite what you might think.' His dark gaze slid to her face, a fleeting glance. 'I certainly have no inclination to tell you what to do.'

Sofia bit down the impulse to take him up on that and run with it. He was just so stubbornly accustomed to dominance, to rejecting without preamble anything he wasn't interested in pursuing—such as an awkward conversation. And yet, he was the first to insist that she always finish what she started. In his own infuriating, endearing way, he was very happy to tell her what to do.

'I'm carrying on with my accountancy work,

as well you know,' she confessed, 'but it's not as important as it once was. The money. The no longer having to work at it. Maybe part of me wants to get into an office environment to test the waters—see whether I'm still energised at the prospect of having a career.'

Rafael's dark eyes glanced across at her. 'That's the problem with money, though, isn't it? It's a blessing but it can also be a curse. Feel free to breathe in the heady fumes of my god-father's offices. At any rate, they're the height of luxury, so perhaps not quite representative of the average office environment. I can't picture you burying yourself behind books and ledgers once this year is up, actually.'

Once this year is up... A tight knot of tension balled in her chest.

'You might be right.' Her voice was non-committal. 'What is happening about Freddy? David doesn't really mention that side of things.'

'I think,' Rafael said, brows knitted as he gave it some thought, 'there might be an element of guilt that things were allowed to slip away from him when he was preoccupied with all his health worries.'

'I never thought of that, but you might be right.'

'I'm always right.' He shot her a sideways glance, full of laughter, and she relaxed. This light-hearted banter was what she knew. It was sexy and lazy and, for her at any rate, warmly intimate.

'Except when you're not.' She smiled.

By the time they reached her father's imposing office in West London, she had swept past her unease about where her relationship with her husband was going.

The building was impressive because, Rafael told her, it was a redevelopment of an old government building, the outside of which had been kept true to its period, solid red brick with a certain prison-like appearance that belied the complete modernisation on the inside.

'You're right,' she breathed, taking in the marble and the giant plants and the banks of lifts to one side. 'Nothing like the average office block.'

'Want me to show you around?'

'You have things to do.'

'I'll get Paula to do the honours. David's PA

left when he retired and since then there have been a string of young girls. Paula is the latest in line. I have to stop a deal Freddy has been trying to consolidate before we kiss goodbye to yet more capital. I'll meet you here in an hour and a half.'

She could see that his mind was already on what he had to do, but she didn't have to wait long before Paula came to fetch her. She was five-foot-nothing and as pretty as a doll, with long blonde hair and bright blue eyes that were friendly and cautious at the same time.

She was a good guide, yet there was a caginess there that Sofia couldn't quite put her finger on, but she was too busy breathing in the place to pay much attention to that.

One entire section was devoted to the rise of her father's boutique hotel business, with colourful photos of his first hotel all the way through to his last, with Argentina featuring somewhere in the middle. She was peering at an album, recognising one or two places, when she heard a voice behind her.

'Wondered when you would make an appearance, my dear stepsister... Is that what you are?

Hmm…difficult with your being off the scene for such a long time. Hard to know *what* to call you. Somehow, *sis* feels all wrong.'

Sofia turned round to find that Freddy had stolen into the room and shut the door behind him without her having heard him.

He was impeccably dressed and groomed to within an inch of his blond locks, but there was a cruelty in his eyes that she had clocked the very first time she had set eyes on him.

'Freddy.' She offered a stiff smile and remained where she was. Her nerves had kicked in and they went into overdrive as he moved towards her before pausing and then circling her, eyes roving up and down in the process.

'So.' He completed the circle and then stood in front of her. 'David's long-lost daughter. Touching. Can't tell you how surprised we all were.'

'We?'

'Of course!' His eyebrows shot up. 'You didn't think that you could make a grand entrance—*fille prodigue*, no less—without raising a few questions, did you? And no sooner are you here than the big, bad wolf, your newly acquired husband, is rushing along playing trouble shooter. Hmm…now, let me think… perhaps *we* is an overstatement. You're not visible enough to raise any eyebrows. I have to admit that you've given award-winning performances whenever you've been out in the public domain. But, my dear *sis*, you don't fool me.' He sighed elaborately. 'That story of love at first sight…whirlwind romance with Mr Eligible Bachelor dispatched to bring you back to your dear papa… Call me sceptical, but it doesn't wash with me…'

'I think I've seen all there is to see in this room,' Sofia countered politely. 'Paula's waiting for me to carry on with the tour.'

'Sadly, Paula has had to deal with other business. It's just the two of us and, before that nosy, over-zealous so-called husband of yours begins wondering where you are, I should tell you that it's not going to work.'

'I don't know what you're talking about.'

Nosy? Over-zealous? Because he was trying to get a grip on this man's destructive management? Rage boiled inside her but diplomacy won out over emotion.

'He's been running around checking up on some of my decisions and meddling. Probably trying to dig up dirt on me as well, not that he's going to find anything. I'm as pure as the driven snow. And, just putting it out there, I wonder what tongues would start wagging if the rumour somehow started that the loved-up couple was all a fake…? I could spice things up a bit. Shares have a nasty habit of responding to rumours…up one minute, down the next…'

Sofia's lip curled and then, before she knew it, he was so much closer to her, standing right in front of her, and the atmosphere shifted. He reached out and stroked her bare arm. For a few shocking seconds she couldn't react, was catapulted back to a time when the unwanted attention of men had made her heart beat faster with apprehension, then she drew back sharply.

'Feel free to pass the message along, my dearest prodigal stepsister.' He moved away, back towards the door. 'He's wasting his time. I'm here to stay and I intend to get fully involved in running this show, whatever Mr High-and-Mighty may think on the subject. Sooner or later, he'll get bored trying to figure me out, and then he can ride off into the sunset, back to his own company. In the meantime, good luck to him!' He half-saluted, pulled open the door and was gone.

Sofia only realised how tense the interchange had made her when she released one long, in-drawn breath on a shudder. Sure enough, when she got her legs moving and peered out of the room, Paula was no longer around. Sofia had left her outside on a phone call and, yes, she had been dispatched while Freddy had done what he had wanted to do.

Which was what? Warned her to warn Ra-fael? She shivered, because there had been more to that twenty-minute exchange than a simple case of intimidation.

She sped through the rest of the company simply because she happened to be on a tour, even if it was a tour without a guide, and be-cause she refused to be cowed by Freddy.

She'd met types like him before. Maybe with-out the power but he was definitely a *type*.

The thoughts clarified in her head but she had already joined Rafael, left the building and was sitting in a small restaurant with him with a menu in front of her before she said, hesitantly, 'You'll never guess who I bumped into...'

Rafael carefully dropped his menu and re-laxed back in the chair to look at her with brooding intensity.

'I must be psychic because I could sense something was wrong within five seconds of meeting you in the foyer.' He beckoned the waitress across while keeping his eyes pinned to Sofia's face. It was a talent she had noticed he possessed. There was never any need for him to beckon for anyone's attention when they were in a restaurant or a bar. He just seemed to emanate some kind of invisible aura that did the talking for him. Or maybe serving staff had special antennae for guys like him. At any rate, the waitress had tripped over before Sofia had time to launch into what she wanted to say.

'Will I need anything stronger than a glass of wine to deal with what's bugging you?'

'It's no big deal.'

'Tell me.' He ordered a bottle of wine and waited until they had chosen what they wanted and the waitress had vanished. 'Who did you bump into?'

'Freddy.'

Rafael stilled and for a few seconds he didn't say anything. 'Interesting. I was hoping to do the same but he couldn't be located for love nor money. The man has a peculiar talent for evasion when it comes to facing me down. What did that waste of space have to say for himself?'

'Well…' She sat back as a selection of tapas was placed in front of them, light and tasty and perfect for a late lunch. 'For a start, I can tell you that he's not your biggest fan.'

'I think I came to that conclusion a long time ago.'

'Aside from the business with work…and he's very smug that you won't be able to stop him from doing what he wants to do…he also told me that he didn't believe in this, in *us*, and that he might just decide to share that with the rest of the world.'

Rafael regarded her narrowly. 'Quite the conversation the pair of you had. How did this come about, bearing in mind you were supposed to have had a dedicated tour guide showing you the highlights and lowlights of the company?'

'I went to the room where there's a potted history of the company and its expansion. Paula had already shown me around various departments. I left her outside taking a call and the next thing I knew Freddy had entered the room and Paula had disappeared.'

'And I'm thinking that the two things are somehow connected. Did he think that he could use scare tactics on you because he's not man enough to face me himself?'

Sofia didn't say anything. She realised, with some surprise, that she had nibbled away at most of the little dishes and drunk a glass of wine. Her mind had been a million miles away.

'Do you plan on returning to David's company after this?'

'I hadn't planned on it. You haven't answered my question, Sofia. Did the man frighten you in any way?'

'We weren't having a conversation in a dark alley miles away from anyone.' She tried to laugh but, thinking about it, he *had* creeped her out.

Rafael leant forward and took both her hands in his. The gesture was so tender and so unsolicited that her heart leapt inside her and she felt that *thing* again, the thing she cautioned herself against—a feeling of being *cared for* somehow.

She knew that it was an illusion but that was where hope always broke free and did its own thing. Hope that all her cynicism might one day be proved wrong. Hope that he would realise that, in the end, she was more, than a business transaction.

They made love, they talked, she made him laugh on occasion…they *communicated*…and then there were these instances of tenderness, a tenderness she knew he didn't even realise he was indulging. Surely all of that must amount to *something*?

Sofia knew that that was why she just kept on hoping. Kept on hoping that he was interested in a whole lot more than just sex, if only he could see it with his eyes wide open.

'Not the point,' he was telling her now, his eyes pinning her to the spot. 'Did he frighten you?'

'What would you do if I told you that he

had?' she returned lightly, but then she wondered what she would achieve by mentioning that he *had* made the hairs on the back of her neck stand on end, and if that wasn't a certain amount of fear then what was? 'He didn't, as it happens. Men like Freddy don't scare me.'

'Men like Freddy? Join the dots for me, Sofia.'

'He...yes, he did waffle on a bit about you wasting your time rooting around for something to use against him, and I got the feeling that he was probably telling the truth. He might not be too bright but he's bright enough to know that anything fraudulent would spell the end of his career at my father's company, however many shares he was given in the divorce settlement.'

'He's read the fine print,' Rafael said thoughtfully. 'And you may well be right. I've shot down a few dead ends, even when I've smelled something fishy, something that might have compromised our man. All I've got to show for my hard work is a trail of semi-incompetence and a lot of shuffling and wheedling and machinations to get rid of people who might be inclined to block his crazy ideas and install a bunch of no-hopers who would do whatever he asked them to.' He shrugged. 'I might have to resign myself to taking what has been signed over to me and then just keeping a watchful eye on the rest. Damage limitation.'

He sighed with frustration and she could read him so well by now that she knew where that frustration stemmed from. He had assumed he would be able to sort everything out in record time and to find that his efforts might well result in nothing would make his pearly whites snap together in rage. He loathed Freddy, thought he was sly and devious and ultimately capable of ruining the company David had built. Maybe not overnight, but incompetence would eat at the foundations and eventually the whole structure would topple to the ground. And would Rafael be able to stop that? It would be a full-time task and he had his own massive empire to run. Time was not his friend.

'There *is* something, though, Rafael,' Sofia told him quietly. She sipped some water and then, when plates had been cleared away, she leaned towards him, elbows on the table, hands clasped, fingers entwined. 'He... I'm not sure how to say this…but he touched me. Please don't think that he *frightened* me, because he *didn't*, but he did touch me.'

The silence that greeted this was so deep and so dense that a shiver of apprehension raced up and down her spine. Rafael's face was inscrutable but his eyes were narrowed and for a few seconds she was privy to a vision of the ruthless steel that lay beneath the velvet glove.

'Not,' she repeated, 'in any way that was scary. He just ran his fingers on my arm.' She laughed but Rafael didn't return the laugh and his body language was so taut and still that she wanted to demand to know what was going through his head.

'Did he now?'

There was a sickness rising up inside Rafael that he barely recognised. He clenched his fists and controlled a powerful and bewildering urge to punch something. Was this what jealousy tasted like? No, couldn't be. He'd never been jealous before. He'd gone out with women who graced the catwalk, and commanded second, third and fourth looks wherever they went, and he'd never had a problem with that. And if some guy had made a pass at any of them? He'd certainly never felt this roar of rage inside him, this pounding in his head and throbbing in his temples.

Was it because she was his wife? Maybe it was because of that. In name only but perhaps he was more of a dinosaur than he'd ever imagined and the fact that he was married to her had evoked some kind of primal, possessive streak he'd never experienced. That surely must be it?

He thought of Freddy, pictured that weak face, his manicured hand on her arm and one thought ran though his head—he was going to sort him out one way or another. Things had just got personal.

Sofia tugged his hand gently so that he was once again looking directly at her and she could judge something of his thoughts in his stunning dark gaze. He was clever at keeping concealed what he had no intention of revealing, but she had to try and read his expression, and she wasn't going to do that if he was looking away.

'When I said that I'd met men like Freddy before I wasn't kidding. The way I look...?'

She rolled her eyes with self-deprecation, because it was always embarrassing to discuss her looks. She'd been accused, nastily, of vanity too many times as a teenager, and had learned to shy away from drawing attention to her appearance. Blending into the background had been one of her greatest aims. 'Men have always thought that they could try it on but I learned how to separate the wheat from the chaff at a very young age. Most guys are obvious but the ones to watch out for are the ones who sneak up from behind and Freddy is one of those. He's a sneaker-upper kind of guy.'

She paused and then took a deep breath. 'He might not be guilty of out-and-out embezzlement or whatever but you should try talking to some of the young girls who work in the company.'

Rafael was staring at her and she could see the dawning comprehension in his eyes. He said, in a low voice, 'Tell me more, my darling. I'm all ears.'

My darling...

For a few seconds, Sofia lost track of what she had been saying. He'd called her his darling. Not *cara*, but *darling*, and she thrilled inside. Then she collected her thoughts and licked her lips, thinking of the best way to say what she had to say.

'I think he might be more than just an office pest. He's a guy who has a lot of power within that company and, from everything you and David have said, he's been systematically getting rid of the old-school employees who might have had the wherewithal to stand up to him. Have you had a look at the girls in the main admin department?'

Rafael slowly shook his head. 'I don't tend to venture down there,' he murmured. 'I've been too busy dealing with the books to see whether any cooking has been going on. Too busy trying to stall ill-conceived deals that should never have kicked off in the first place. I've really only had dealings with the CEOs.'

'They're all young and attractive,' Sofia said bluntly. 'And a lot of them have only been there a short while.'

'I'm joining the dots.' He looked at her thoughtfully but he wasn't *looking* at her. His mind was somewhere else. Sofia could see that.

Then he was looking at her again, eyes sombre. 'You said you were accustomed to men like Freddy,' he murmured. 'By that you mean seedy creeps who have tried to prey on you?'

Sofia looked away and shrugged. 'It's life.'

'Any of them succeed in doing what you tell me Freddy didn't do?'

'What do you mean?'

'Any of them frighten you?'

Sofia reddened, suddenly restless and feeling exposed. Opening up was one thing when you were doing it with someone who truly cared about you. It was a different matter when you were revealing yourself to a guy who didn't really care.

But there was something in his voice, a questioning gentleness that pierced right to the very core of her.

'My mother was a very sexy woman. Very beautiful. Men chased after her and sometimes, when they saw me, they thought that I might come as part of the deal. Most just looked. Surreptitiously, making sure my mother didn't notice. She could be a tiger like that. But *I* noticed and always made sure to take evasive action.

But one night…well…there was a party and I was in bed. Someone came into the bedroom.' She shivered, living the memory. 'I was terrified,' she admitted. 'He was disturbed before anything could happen but I always knew that that was luck on my side and if luck had been busy somewhere else…'

Rafael reached out and took her hand in his, linking fingers. 'Shh…' His voice was low and persuasive. 'That time has passed. You're here with me now. Safe.'

Her eyes flickered to his.

Safe? She almost wanted to laugh. She'd stopped being *safe* with him a long time ago. She'd given her heart and was wandering in alien territory and, the last thing she was was *safe*. If only he knew…

CHAPTER NINE

SOFIA WAS BASKING in the warm glow of David's satisfaction. It was writ large in the quiet pleasure in his eyes. He had peppered her with all sorts of interesting anecdotes about some of the people at the company and about deals long done when he had been climbing the ladder of success.

Sofia listened, quietly marvelling at how far their relationship had come. She had been so antagonistic to start with, so convinced that there could be no meeting ground between them, no place where they could join hands and look to any kind of future without the past being a stealthy, toxic intruder. How wrong she had been. She was guiltily aware that she should have had a bit more faith in her mother who would not have given her heart so completely to someone who wasn't worth the gift. She had never loved again, even though she had carried on searching for love, and it was as though she had lost her compass, choosing all the wrong kinds of guys, desperately becoming a woman who relied on her looks to find her what she was looking for.

She wondered what she would tell David about her visit to the company because looking around had not been the straightforward meet-and-greet she had anticipated, interrupted as it had been by Freddy and his threatening behaviour. But she had selectively decided to omit that aspect of her visit and concentrate, instead, on her genuine delight at seeing where everything had started all those years ago.

Freddy and what was going to happen to him was something she had left at Rafael's door. Certainly, after her revelations, Rafael had looked like a man on a mission. She would have felt sorry for the younger man if she hadn't known, in her gut, just how much of a creep Freddy could turn out to be—*already was.*

She sneaked a surreptitious glance at her watch, already counting down to when she would see Rafael. In front of her was an assortment of cakes but she wasn't going to fill up on them because she had cooked earlier and would be eating dinner with Rafael when she was back at the house a bit later.

'Tell me what you thought of the History Room,' David was saying excitedly, fussing and bustling and pouring her another cup of tea.

'I loved it.' Sofia smiled. 'I think it's very inspirational to have photos of all the hotels and all the work that went into them framed for your employees to see.'

'Rafael's idea, don't you know.'

'Was it?' She leaned forward with interest. Every word uttered about Rafael was of interest to her. She had gleaned so many titbits over time—had gone through old photo albums, taking her time, with Rafael sitting next to her, amused by her fascination, telling David that lengthy chats about youthful nonsense wasn't of interest to man nor beast. She had almost no photos of herself.

'Oh, yes,' David was saying. 'Years ago. He was busy trying to get his own house in order after his parents were killed but still had time to think about me when I was redesigning the headquarters when I bought over the building next door. Sort of chap he is, but I expect you've reached that conclusion yourself.'

'Conclusion?'

'I've seen you two together, my dear.' He sat and gazed longingly at the plate of morsels and sighed with resignation when she wagged a finger at him, warning him off eating more than the two he had already had.

'What do you mean?'

'The way you are together. The way you interact.' He looked at her with satisfaction. He waved one hand, brushing off some distant point in the past he no longer considered relevant. 'I know that as marriages went this was perhaps not the sort you had ever envisaged for yourself, my dear girl, but I sense that what started out as an arrangement may well have taken wings.'

Sofia was enjoying this, a guilty sort of enjoyment, because every word was music to her ears. If David had noticed a change in the relationship she and Rafael shared, then surely there was something there?

'What do you mean?' she prompted, and

David shot her a sly, all-knowing look from under his bushy eyebrows.

'Never seen him like this before,' he confessed. 'Not with any of those women he's dated in the past. Sure, you're *married*, but we both know that that was not a real marriage, and yet now...you're both somehow different around one another.'

Sofia could agree with that verdict. The truth was that there was a physical familiarity between them that neither of them ever bothered to conceal. Intimate, passing touches that were very different from the obvious displays of affection they had made sure to demonstrate for the public at the very beginning.

'You know,' David said thoughtfully, 'I can't even remember Rafael being like this with his first wife.'

From a long way away, Sofia was aware that her temperature was dropping, that she was getting as cold as a block of ice. She could almost feel her vital organs slowing down as she wrestled to make sense of what had just been said.

David was bustling again, the way he did, lifting the lid of the teapot, looking at the dainty bell on the table as though debating whether to summon 'the old dragon', as he fondly referred to his live-in nurse.

'Yes…first wife…'

'Gemma. Must have told you about her?'

Sofia's head was spinning. Suddenly hearing about a wife she'd known nothing about was something she didn't want to come from her father's lips. It felt as though she had stumbled on a stash of secret love letters, buried deep, stored where they were destined never to be found.

'Gemma…'

As a real wife, this was something she would already have known about, but a real wife she wasn't—even though she had been lulled into thinking that somehow she had turned into one.

She had to go. Had to think and clear her head. She leapt to her feet and for a few seconds stared in silence at a startled David, while she tried to think of a suitable excuse for flying out like a bat out of hell.

'I've—I've suddenly remembered,' she stammered lamely. 'I have an appointment…with… with the dentist!'

'You have?'

'The cakes have reminded me! A filling needs seeing to before it becomes...er...'

What was the next step after a filling anyway? Wasn't a filling the last thing that happened after a toothache?

'Painful.' David looked concerned, which immediately made her feel guilty.

'I'm really sorry, Dad.'

They both stared at one another at that slip of the tongue.

'David.'

'You can call me Dad,' he returned gruffly. 'And shoo! Call me when you're next coming over.'

She didn't go directly back to Rafael's house. He wouldn't have been back at any rate. Instead, head in a daze, she trekked through London, soaking up an atmosphere she had very quickly taken for granted. Everyone was in a hurry. The pavements were packed: shoppers... people hurrying out of offices because it had gone six...tourists drifting without a care in the world, getting in the way...

She'd changed over the months. It wasn't just

the clothes, the trappings of great wealth. It was *her*. Something deep inside her had changed. She had become confident in a way she'd never been and it wasn't just because she could afford stuff. It was because Rafael had made her so. He had allowed her to be herself and had encouraged her to shed the defensiveness that had once been part and parcel of her personality.

He had made her feel secure.

What a joke.

He knew her inside out and she had kidded herself into thinking that she knew him as well, even if he couldn't see it, even if his stubborn pride prevented him from accepting it.

She didn't know him at all and that felt like a crushing blow. She wandered in and out of shops before heading back to his place a little after eight.

He was already there when she quietly let herself in. He'd obviously been waiting for her to show up because he was in the hall before she had time to sling her jacket over the banister.

'I've been calling,' was the first thing he said, moving towards her.

'Have you?' Sofia dodged past him and headed straight into the kitchen. 'I'm sorry. I haven't looked at my phone at all.' She heard a tell-tale hitch in her voice and cautioned herself against giving in to self-pity. So she was here, stripped bare of all her illusions, and she only had herself to blame. He'd never promised her more than he could deliver and if she'd hoped for more then that was her fault.

Love had been a handicap, making her question less, demand less and accept more.

'David said that you had some kind of emergency appointment with the dentist?'

'I haven't been to the dentist, Rafael.' She spun round on her heels and looked at him, arms folded, eyes cool.

Rafael stared back, hesitant.

What was going on here? Astute as he was at reading situations, he was finding it difficult to get a grip. As a general rule, he had no time for any sort of hysterical behaviour. He didn't like confrontations or arguments, preferring to walk away from histrionics, and this was shaping up to be all of the above mentioned. Judging from her expression, at least.

'Then where were you?'

'Out. Walking around.'

'Out? Walking around?'

'Thinking.'

Rafael remained silent, a dark flush delineating his aristocratic, high cheekbones.

'Aren't you going to ask me what I was thinking about, Rafael?'

'I expect you're going to tell me whether I ask you or not.'

'I found something out today.' Sofia heard the wobble in her voice and anchored herself firmly back in the reality of what she was dealing with—a guy who, in the end, cared so little for her that he hadn't seen fit to tell her about what had probably been the biggest thing in his life to date.

Had it been a happy marriage? Sad? Disappointing? Something in between all three? How long had it lasted? Had it been love at first sight? What had she looked like? What had happened in the end?

She had asked David none of those questions, had not wanted to know any details at all except the ones that came from Rafael. Was she overreacting? She didn't think she was, although some might. As far as she was concerned, this revelation felt like the summing up of everything she'd feared—that this wonderful, complex, infuriating, adorable and strangely vulnerable man felt no real attachment to her. Yes, he wanted her, but that was never going to be enough. And, yes, he liked her well enough but that didn't touch the surface of what she wanted him to feel. She'd been greedy and this was the price she was now having to pay.

The truth was that, if he had had the connection with her that she had with him, he would have confided in her, slotted in that piece of the jigsaw puzzle that was such an important part of the whole picture. That was how relationships worked, wasn't it? Had she found out sooner about this, maybe it would have been different. She might have been able to ease it into the conversation and excuse his reticence on the grounds that they were still finding a way forward with one another, still learning to have a relationship within the confines of their convenient marriage. But to find out when she thought that what they had was something special was truly painful.

'David mentioned that you've been married once before.' She didn't bother beating about the bush.

The silence settled between them, suffocating and dense, becoming more and more uncomfortable with each passing second. The shutters had snapped down and his expression, his stunning dark eyes that had warmed when they rested on her, were as remote now as the cold, grey waters of a wintry sea.

'He thought I would have known,' she laboured on. 'Of course, that was the first I was hearing of any such thing. I didn't ask for details. I... I couldn't. I thought those details would be better coming from you.'

Rafael's gaze narrowed, his lean, darkly handsome face betraying immediate and instinctive rejection of what he viewed as a blunt battering ram aimed against his privacy. Things had been going so well between them that this felt like an attack out of the blue and, as with all attacks, his initial reaction was to repel. Taut with frustrated tension, he was at a loss as to the direction he should take, but the mere thought of having to explain himself to her or to anyone was like a drawbridge being slammed down.

Some things had the power to change the course of a person's life and his brief and disastrous marriage had been one of those things. He'd been a fool, had been sucked in by a gold-digger and had managed to get out of it in one piece. End of story. Being called upon to revisit that intensely disillusioning and personal slice of his past evoked a primitive, negative response and a searing resentment that the matter had been raised at all. Gut reaction bypassed common sense.

'What do you want me to say, Sofia? It was something that happened. That was then and this is now and I don't see the relevance of digging into the past.'

'You *don't see the relevance* of digging into the past?' Sofia exploded, storming towards him, every nerve in her body reacting with rage at his casual dismissal of something she considered perfectly reasonable. She had had a couple of hours to think the thing through and there was now a seething mass of hurt and pain roiling inside her. Casual dismissal of what she was feeling just wasn't going to cut it.

'We're sleeping together, Rafael! I think a certain amount of meaningful conversation is to be expected!'

Rafael clenched his fists, fighting down the urge to reach out, pull her towards him and sort things out the most effective way he knew how. Face to face, naked body pressed against naked body, his mouth on hers, silencing all those intrusive questions he was not inclined to answer.

For a few seconds, something rushed through him, a hesitation that was unlike anything he had ever felt before. It was unsettling, disconcerting. Why, he wondered, was he so anchored in a desire for privacy? She was making a simple enough request that required a simple enough answer. Where was the harm in relenting? He remembered Gemma and the unravelling of juvenile dreams—remembered what it felt like to know that someone was using you. He'd made sure to protect himself from ever going down that road again. He'd made himself invulnerable. As far as he was concerned, confession was never good for the soul.

Never. Age-old defences and behaviour patterns killed all uncomfortable hesitation stone-dead.

'There's nothing to tell, Sofia. It happened and I just don't see the value in dredging it up. Things didn't work out between us. I was young, too young to see the pitfalls. Unfortunately.'

'That's it?'

'What do you mean?' He frowned, incredulous that another onslaught might be in the making.

One sentence! The briefest of explanations! Plus it had been like drawing blood from a stone.

It didn't matter whether he found it hard to discuss feelings or whether he'd put the past to bed and wasn't interested in resurrecting it. The fact was that she was owed more than this. Furthermore, if she accepted this and overlooked it, she would set a precedent that could never be broken—a precedent of always having to keep quiet about anything troublesome he might not be interested in hearing.

Even if he yielded sufficiently to want longer together, even if he admitted that there was more to their relationship than convenience and sex, was this the sort relationship she was after? For herself? Long-term?

'Nothing. I don't mean anything.' She swerved away and clattered around for a few seconds, getting her thoughts together. Calm was settling over her.

She wasn't going to rant and rave. She heated the food in silence and was dimly aware of him sitting at the table, watching her, dark eyes alert, speculative. But notably he wasn't going near any more thorny issues. It seemed that awkward silence was a lot more comfortable than questions he didn't want to answer.

'You're not eating.' He stated the obvious when there was a plate of food in front of him. 'Are you sulking?' He pushed the plate away from him and sat back, hands linked on his chest, watching her in a way that could still set her pulses racing even though she couldn't have been angrier or more miserable than she was just at the moment.

Sofia thought it typical of Rafael to reduce her very valid concerns to a simple case of *sulking*.

'Sofia.' He raked his hands through his hair and vaulted upright, prowling towards her so that she backed away until she was pressed up against the counter, at which point she resolutely folded her arms, forming a barrier between them, and stared at him. His eyes were a hot spot so she looked a bit lower, only to realise that his mouth was also a hot spot. She gazed past his shoulder and tried to remain neutral and stony-faced.

'You haven't eaten,' was all Rafael could find to say.

'I've lost my appetite. Rafael, I think I need to take time out on…on us. On this.'

'What?'

His expression would have been comical if she had been in the mood for laughing.

'I'm going to go upstairs.' Stunned silence. 'To pack.'

'Sofia, is all this about me not wanting to

wallow in long explanations about a relationship I had a lifetime ago? Jesus, this is *ridiculous*!'

'I don't want to listen to this. You don't have to talk about your past, Rafael, but likewise I don't have to put up with your silence on the subject.'

'You're being illogical!'

Sofia swerved past him, out of reach, and walked quickly towards the door. When she glanced back, it was to find him staring at her as though she had taken leave of her senses.

There was so much she wanted to say to him that she wouldn't have known where to begin. If she started, she would never stop. There was an angry, hurting roar inside her that had to be contained because she didn't want to descend into being the sort of shrieking, hysterical woman she was so close to being.

'This marriage has done what it was supposed to do,' she said neutrally.

'What the hell do you mean by that?'

'I *mean*, Rafael, that I've built a bridge with my father. We no longer need you as an intermediary. And as for Freddy? I'm pretty sure you'll sort that business out because if my suspicions about him are correct, and I'm pretty sure they are, you'll have a powerful incentive for him to listen to what you have to say. Weren't those the reasons behind this convenient marriage?'

Their eyes met and she didn't look away.

He was so spectacular on so many fronts, she thought weakly. How had she ever been so stupid as to think that she could protect herself against the sheer force of his dangerous, vital charisma? He was a stalking panther to her inexperienced gazelle.

'My aunt and Miguel have moved closer to the hospital where he's having his treatments,' she intoned, 'and their house is more than big enough for me for a while. And after that I have options, Rafael. I'll work out what to do next. But I won't be doing it as your wife.'

CHAPTER TEN

OPTIONS? *OPTIONS?* WHAT options was she going to consider? Rafael stared at the empty space she'd left behind her and tried to marshal his thoughts.

She was his wife and she was walking out on their marriage! That was the first furious thought that sprang into his head but immediately he had to concede that she had a point because this hadn't started life as any sort of marriage anyone would call *conventional*. Unfortunately, her brutal assessment of it as a business arrangement jarred. He should have been the first to agree with the description, but the fact that it jarred did all sorts of things to his peace of mind.

What was going on?

They'd made love! Fantastic, mind-blowing, amazing love, so why was he sitting here alone in this kitchen wondering what the hell was going on?

He pushed the plate of food further away, determined that he wasn't going to do the unthinkable and follow her up the stairs. If she wanted to walk out, then that was fine. Nothing he could do about it. This was never meant to be have been a permanent state of affairs anyway!

More to the point, he had no time for the sort of ridiculous behaviour she had just displayed. God knew, what did it matter whether he'd been married for five minutes a hundred years ago? Why couldn't she see that? Why were women so incomprehensible? It was particularly disappointing with her because she knew him so well! Better than any woman had ever known him! Indeed, no one had ever come close. They might have started off facing each other from opposite sides of the ring but they had gradually closed the distance, become a team.

She had cornered him and then she had decided to stand her ground, and what that amounted to was some kind of ultimatum and he'd never been one to do ultimatums.

Unnerved by thoughts and feelings that were alien to him, Rafael leapt to his feet, walked jerkily towards the kitchen window to stare outside.

Had she finished her packing? There wasn't much to pack. He knew that because her clothes were laid out alongside his in the same wardrobe, same shelves, same drawers. He couldn't care less what got flung behind doors, but she was as neat as a pin, and was forever folding his clothes into submission. Black T-shirts in tidy stacks, boxers rolled, socks in a drawer of their own.

When had she started organising him and how was it that he was only now noticing?

He rarely ate dinner without her. Business dos...yes, there had been a few. But he had bailed on a lot more than usual because he preferred her company. He liked hearing about her days. She made him laugh. She'd made friends with some of the women in the village. There was always gossip. She had a way of telling him what was going on that never failed to make him smile. His custom of always working if he happened to be in in the evenings had long been abandoned. There were now better things to do with his time. All those things, he now realised, involved *her* and not all of them had to do with sex.

Agitated, Rafael half-wished he could shut the box that had suddenly been opened—hold back the river of thoughts pouring through his head, undammed for the first time.

What the hell were those so-called options she was going to consider? Argentina was waiting for her. Her aunt and cousin were in a luxurious place just outside Buenos Aires. He had seen some photos on her phone only a couple of weeks ago. And then what? Divorce? Was that one of the options she had mentioned? And thereafter the unknown opened up, gaping like a dark void waiting to be filled. Frankly, the world would be her oyster, because she had more money than she could shake a stick at.

Unbelievably wealthy, unbelievably sexy and unbelievably single…

Rafael's blood ran cold when he thought of where that lethal combination would lead.

He didn't stop to think himself out of anything. He slammed out of the kitchen, bolted up the stairs and pushed open the bedroom door before his usual stubborn pride could begin telling him what he should or shouldn't do.

In the act of dumping the last of her things into one of the three cases she had fetched from where they had been languishing in one of the spare rooms, Sofia had zero expectations that Rafael would try and talk her out of her decision to leave him.

If she knew anything about him by now, it was that he never pursued. She had dumped him and there was no way that he was going to try and talk her out of it.

And there was certainly no way that she could turn the clock back and pretend that words spoken had not been aired.

She'd made her bed and now she was going to have to lie on it, and it was looking pretty grim. Beyond grim. Unbearable. Of course, she knew that this was where she was meant to be—and she didn't regret starting the conversation that had brought her here because she'd needed *honesty*—but the proverbial bed was still looking terrifying, cold and empty.

She stared down at the suitcase, startled to see that her usual orderly packing had given way to a free-for-all of clothes hurled indiscriminately into the case. Her head was so full of riotous thoughts that she couldn't seem to separate them, couldn't deal with them one at a time. Maybe if she could she wouldn't be standing here feeling sick and dizzy.

She'd just said goodbye to the only guy she would ever love. He didn't even know how she felt. He just knew that she had turned into a demanding shrew and, that being the case, he had slammed down the shutters, stuck up the 'No Trespass' sign, and bolted the front door.

Try as she might to tell herself that that was fine, because loving a man who couldn't even be bothered to share his past with you was a recipe for disaster, she still felt sick to the stomach.

No more Rafael. No more of those dark, dark eyes teasing her, caressing her, understanding her. She was on her own now and she was as adrift as a castaway at sea.

She jerked up at the sound of the door being

pushed open, slamming against the wall, and then gaped as he stood there staring at her.

Every single self-defence mechanism she possessed slammed into place. Had a sense of pity got the better of him? Had he decided that she might deserve some kind of bracing pep talk now that she was on her way? After all, she *had* been instrumental in David getting back on his feet and finding things to look forward to, not to mention sorting out the whole troublesome business of Freddy. Had he decided that she was due something a bit more than a flat refusal to indulge her perfectly normal curiosity?

'What do you want?' she asked, breaking eye contact and turning away to begin the process of flinging underwear into her suitcase.

'Sofia...'

'What?' She clicked her tongue impatiently and spun around to stare at him, hands on her hips.

'You asked a question back there in the kitchen,' Rafael said roughly, 'and I should have answered it.'

'It doesn't matter.'

'Well, clearly it does, considering you're

packing to leave me because you didn't get the answer you wanted.'

'There was no *answer I wanted*! No right or wrong way of responding! Just something more than you waving your hand and swatting me away! So don't you *dare* try and lay the blame for this at my door, Rafael.'

'I wasn't aware that I was doing that.' He raked his fingers through his hair and walked into the bedroom to drag the chair by the dressing table across to the window and there he proceeded to watch her as she continued her packing. He didn't sit still for long. He stood up and walked to the dressing table, picking up random stuff and repositioning them. Her hairbrush. A magnifying mirror. A lipstick. It was disconcerting and she found that she couldn't carry on doing what she was doing while he was behaving so…weirdly.

'Anyway,' she muttered, 'It doesn't matter. I shouldn't have asked.' Her mouth twisted in a semblance of a sarcastic smile. 'It was way beyond my brief to ever think that you might have seen fit to share something as huge about your past as a marriage. What a fool I was, forgetting that I was just your business partner!'

'Don't.'

'Don't what?'

'Be sarcastic. It doesn't suit you.'

'Oh, dear. Well, I'd better listen and obey that command. Except...why should I? I'm leaving you so I don't actually have to listen or obey anything you say.'

'You never have.' Rafael perched against the dressing table and folded his arms but his usual air of self-assured cool was missing.

He looked...*rattled*.

Before she could start analysing what *that* meant, she flung open the wardrobe doors and stared down at an array of shoes befitting the woman she had become but certainly not the woman she had once been.

For some reason, the sight brought tears to her eyes and she remained very still for a few seconds, eyes downcast, before gathering herself and sifting through the shoes to remove a pair of trainers and a pair of walking boots. She didn't think she'd be needing stilettoes or designer slip-ons again. Her next step forward was back to Argentina, back to where she belonged, where she would take stock, and then maybe see a bit of the world. Travel was good for the soul, and although she wouldn't be travelling like a princess, with a trunk of fancy shoes and fancy ball gowns, neither would she be heading forth without knowing where she would be sleeping when nightfall rolled around.

'It's what I've always liked about you.'

His deep voice was so close behind her that she actually jumped and then spun around to find that he had managed to creep up on her without making a sound. How could a big guy move so silently? She inched back and he made no move to close the tiny gap between them. He just stared down at her with an expression that she couldn't begin to read but which was as unnerving as his lack of cool.

'Yes, I was once married. I was young...'

'You don't have to.' She looked away, red-faced, heart beating like a sledgehammer. 'In a fake marriage no one has a right to confidences and, if I chose to confide in you, then you didn't ask for any of it.'

'You have a right,' Rafael said seriously. 'To know.'

'I have no idea what you're trying to say, Rafael, and I can't deal with riddles. Not right now.'

'I'm being straight with you.' There was the ghost of a tremor in his voice and she pretended not to notice, because she knew that to notice would just open the door to all those stupid questions in her head, and she knew from bitter experience that those questions never led anywhere she wanted to go.

'Not only do you have every right to be curious about my past but I have absolutely no right to deny you whatever answers you want. In fact, I should have told you about my marriage. God knows, there were enough opportunities, because what we had, the relationship that unfolded between us, stopped being about a business arrangement a long time ago.' He cupped the side of her face with his hand and she didn't jerk back. 'You confided in me and it should have been natural for me to return the favour.'

'You were never going to do that, Rafael,' she

said brusquely. 'You have always made it very clear that you don't do the touchy-feely stuff.'

'I know,' he admitted freely. 'And therein lay the problem.' He shot her a crooked smile that rocked her from the inside out and made her pulses race, and her heart speed up just a little bit more.

The atmosphere between them was electric and she didn't want to break it. Asking him to carry on because she was riveted risked breaking it so she remained silent, staring at him, eyes as wide as saucers.

'I've never confided in anyone, and old habits die hard. David is about the only person on the face of the earth who has ever had the ability to make me do anything I may not have wanted to do.'

'I know. I get that. He asked you to go to Argentina to check me out and I don't suppose you ever really thought that you might turn down the request.'

'He gave me purpose. My parents had no time for me. He did. I owe him.' He shifted on his feet and slid his gaze over to the bed. 'This is a…difficult conversation for me. Maybe difficult isn't quite the right word. What I'm saying is that I'd rather we had it on more...neutral territory.'

'Are you feeling all right?' Sofia asked sharply. 'If you have anything awkward to say to me then I'd rather you just come out and say it, although I can't imagine there's anything you could say that might bring on a fainting fit.'

She thought there was no place lower to where she could be tossed than the place she was currently occupying—a place where he would no longer be playing a part, leaving her to make her way forward on her own. She had thought that he would become dependent on her without realising it. She had failed to take into account that that was a plan that could work both ways and now, looking into an empty future, she realised that *she* was the one who had become increasingly dependent on *him*. *She* was the one who now felt as though they should be a team and, left on her own, had no idea how she was going to cope. *She* was the one who had become vulnerable and defenceless in the long run.

'Let's go downstairs. Aside from anything else, I need a stiff drink.'

'I want to pack and leave.'

'Please, Sofia.'

She wavered and then nodded. 'Okay, but…'

'I get it. But I need you to hear me out. Please.' He spun on his heels and made for the door, then down the stairs into the sitting room, which was a sanctuary of cool shades, deep-pile carpet and comfortable sofas. No leather or glass or chrome in sight.

'Well?' She folded her arms and stared at him as he prowled through the room before sinking into one of the chairs and crossing his legs. He nodded to her, indicating that she should do likewise, and after a few seconds she did.

Instead of picking up where he had left off, however, Rafael stood up, choosing to join her on the chair, which was a generous two-seater. He couldn't keep still. She had never seen him like that, as though he was at odds with his body, restless, fidgety and uncomfortable in his skin. It was enough to get past the rational part of her that was telling her to clear off as fast as she could.

'I don't want to talk to you across the width of this room. And what I was saying... Sofia, my darling, I should have told you about Gemma.'

'Wife number one?'

Darling? Did he just call me 'darling' or did I mishear?

Sofia wasn't sure she wanted the details, now that there was a chance that she could be given them. In fact, she wanted to place her hand firmly over his beautiful mouth and stop him from telling her about the one and only love of his life. 'You don't have to tell me anything,' she protested weakly.

'I do,' Rafael said flatly. 'Because it seems that you've got hold of the wrong end of the stick.' He sighed and she could tell that he was trying to work out what to say, how to express feelings, how to emote. For a man as resolutely private and tight-lipped as he was, this was a huge step, and she couldn't stop the skip of hope that filtered through the barriers she had busily been erecting.

What if...? What if...? What if...?

Silence, again, seemed the best way forward. Silence and focusing on her hands, which were resting limply on her lap. That way, there was no danger of him reading anything in her eyes.

'My parents...' He smiled crookedly, his expression acknowledging that he was about to break the mould and go where he had never gone before. 'They were unbelievably irresponsible. You know that, though, because you seem to know all there is to know about me. I must have been blind not to have seen the signs and that's a very big one. But at the risk of boring you with repetition...'

'You could never do that,' she whispered under her breath, eyes finally locking to his, because she just *had* to see his face, *had* to try and gauge what he was thinking from his expression, which was as open as she had ever seen.

'They couldn't cope with having a kid and they were never really interested in trying. To their credit, they made sure not to have more than one, but my childhood was a peripatetic one. I wanted for nothing, because I was the product of two enormously wealthy families, but on an emotional level David was the only person ever to be there for me. Boarding school rescued me from a nomadic life but there were obvious downsides.'

He grimaced. 'I learned to be independent from a very young age, to rely on no one. My parents flitted in and out of my life but by the time I hit my teens I knew better than to ever think that I could bank on them. Promises were made but never kept and anything and everything seemed a better option than being stuck with the grind of parental duties.'

Sofia wasn't aware of reaching out to cover his hand with hers, nor was she aware of him allowing her hand to remain there, accepting the show of sympathy without biting sarcasm and instant rejection. Yes, over time David had confided, and without even realising it so had Rafael, but this was different. This was Rafael *communicating* on a level he had always sworn was beyond his reach.

'By the time they died, I was completely self-sufficient but still young and suddenly I was in charge of what was left of their fortune. A great deal had been squandered, and investments had been made that had further drained the coffers, but I was rich and a target. Too young to be as cynical as I should have been. I was just in my early twenties and fell for a woman who was ten years older than me. I thought it was love. In retrospect, I was obviously searching for someone or something to take me through the bleak period after my parents died. Gemma slotted into that spot and she knew just how to stack the deck.'

Just the thought of Rafael imagining himself to be in love was hurtful and Sofia felt the muscles in her face stiffen and tense as she tried to control her expression.

'How did you meet her?' Sofia eventually asked.

'She was a teacher—and don't look so shocked. I'm not as shallow as you like to imagine. We met in a pub. She was there with a group of her friends and I was there on my own, staring down into a whisky, if memory serves me, and dwelling on a past I wished had been different. Dark thoughts.

'She approached me. I was a regular there. I'll never know if she asked Joe behind the bar who I was, or if it was just fortuitous, an opportunity that arose and one she couldn't resist. Certainly afterwards I remember thinking that she'd sized me up pretty quickly...asked all the right questions...knew that I wasn't just another kid who had to do weekend jobs to afford a pint on the weekend.'

'You're so cautious now...so guarded and defensive. It's hard to imagine...'

'That I was young enough to be stupid?' He smiled. 'I was. But she came with all the right qualities and she knew how to enhance them to her advantage. Compassionate, understanding and...hot. She was the archetypal teenage boy's dream woman, and I was barely out of my teens and ripe for the picking, given what I was going through at the time. I never stopped to look any deeper than what I saw on the outside. David warned me, as it happens...'

'He met her?'

'Of course, and he told me that I should be careful, but I wisely chose to ignore his advice.' Rafael looked at her ruefully. 'To my cost. I married her and the whole sorry episode lasted under six months. Would have lasted longer and cost a lot more if David hadn't taken it upon himself to have her comprehensively checked out.'

'What do you mean?'

'He was still very much on the ball in those days and he always put my best interests ahead of everything. He didn't tell me what he was up to, just had her checked out and presented me with the findings. Turned out she had never stopped sleeping with the boyfriend she'd had when she met me. I was a good catch. Young, rich and, at the time, emotionally unstable. I fell straight into her honey trap.'

'You of all people.' Sofia imagined a vulnerable young Rafael and wished that she had known him then, wished that she had known the boy who had become the man.

'I'm taking that as a compliment. As it turns out, by the time I was presented with all the facts, including the fact that the boyfriend was very much still a presence in her life, I had already realised that love was the last thing I felt for the woman. I got rid of her but it was an ugly, drawn-out business that ended up costing me a fortune—but not, as I've said, nearly as much as it would have done if David hadn't decided to be proactive and take the bull by the horns.'

'No wonder you're so attached to him. He's always had your back.'

'The only one to. Sofia...' He paused and their eyes tangled, and she released a little sigh of helplessness.

'I thought I'd learned how to protect myself. I thought I was immune to the dangers of getting in too deep with any woman, but I didn't know what love was, and I should have had the courage to tell you that when you asked instead of letting you believe that my marriage was something it most certainly was not. I didn't know what love was, and after Gemma I made up my mind that I wasn't going to trust emotions again. Wherever I looked, bloody emotions were always letting the side down. It wasn't just me and my nightmare foray into wedded bliss. My parents were highly emotional, couldn't seem to get the balance right, and David...well... David never recovered from your mother and, as I incorrectly assumed, her desertion. I toughened up and I never thought that the day would come when I would revisit my decision to lock the door on my feelings and throw away the key.'

Sofia found that breathing was becoming difficult. She stared, willing him to continue, and not daring to trust what her eyes and her ears were telling her.

'And you have?' she whispered into the ever-lengthening silence.

'You came along,' Rafael said gravely. 'My convenient wife. Everything changed for me and I didn't even realise that things were changing. Or maybe I did and I subconsciously decided to turn a blind eye because turning a blind eye was the safer option. What started as a sensible arrangement with a timeline turned into the very last thing I expected. I fell in love with you, my darling.'

Sofia closed her eyes. She felt as if she was actually swooning, like a Victorian maiden. When she looked at him, her eyes were bright, although hope was still at war with caution.

'You're not kidding, are you, Rafael?'

'I'm not kidding. I love you. I don't know when it happened. Was it a gradual process? Or did it happen the very instant I first laid eyes on you? All I know is that my life changed the second you entered it. And yet, when you cornered me this evening, all I could do was fall back on the tired old routine of avoiding direct questioning because it was what I had always done. You walked out of that door earlier, *cara*, and I could feel my world falling apart.'

'So was mine.' Her heart was singing. She was giddy with joy. She almost had to pinch herself to believe that the fairy tales she had spun in her head were coming true. Since when did *that* happen?

'I love you too,' she said softly and he smiled.

'I know.'

'You *know*?'

'On some level, I think I've known for quite a while—which was probably why I was so spooked when you tried to pin me down. I knew that it was a crunch moment. I had to make a choice to take what we had beyond the level of just sex, but sex was all I'd ever known when it came to women, and going past that was…bloody terrifying. It didn't matter that I'd crossed that line a long time ago with you.'

Sofia laughed, caressed the side of his face

and then leant forward, tugging him towards her so that she could kiss him. It was somehow different this time. The uncertainty that had plagued her, the hopes and half-formed dreams waiting to be dashed, had been replaced by shining certainty.

'Meeting you was like a bolt from the blue as well for me,' she confessed on a sigh. 'You had your life in order and so did I and I guess both of us, in our own different ways and for our own different reasons, were sceptical about the whole business of falling in love. I definitely never expected to fall for a guy like you. Good-looking, self-assured, alpha male...'

'So many weedy men out there waiting in the wings...' He yanked her towards him and she toppled against him, laughing, loving the feel of his hands moving over her body. 'You'd have eaten them alive.'

'Not sure that's a compliment!'

'It is. Trust me. You're strong and have a mind of your own and it's just one of the many things I love about you.'

'So I guess you could say,' Sofia mused

dreamily, sinking into his arms, 'that the mar-riage of convenience is over?'

'Very definitely over,' Rafael assured her. 'From here on, this marriage is very much for real, and I think we should do something to celebrate that. We did what was necessary at a register office. Now, let's do something more meaningful.' He grinned at her and then kissed the top of her head. 'I'll get David working on that. He's been complaining recently about being bored.'

'I'm sure he'll love planning a fancy meal somewhere!'

'And a blessing. This time round, when I look at you, you're going to know that what we have is for now and for ever. David won't just have gained a long-lost daughter, he will, I very much hope, my darling, be able to look forward to adding to the family tree.'

'I'd like kids.'

'Good. Then I suggest, *cara*, that we get going...right about now...'

* * * * *

LET'S TALK

For exclusive extracts, competitions
and special offers, find us online:

- **f** facebook.com/millsandboon
- **⌾** @millsandboonuk
- **🐦** @millsandboon

Or get in touch on 0844 844 1351*

For all the latest titles coming soon,
visit millsandboon.co.uk/nextmonth